"There's been an accident."

Victoria's corn-gold hair was wild and disheveled, her face was chalk white. The small boy who clung to her hand was on the point of collapse, and his clothing was stained with blood.

Miraculously, they had found their way through the forest to the home of Sir Peter Wycherley. Victoria closed her eyes in relief, but she couldn't shut out the horrible memory of the crash...she was drifting back into a nightmare....

Sir Peter gazed down at her in disbelief. She was the girl who had occupied his dreams, the girl he had been waiting for. But now, it was too late.

OTHER
Harlequin Romances
by SUSAN BARRIE

580—NURSE NOLAN
587—HEART SPECIALIST
628—THE HOUSE OF THE LAIRD
687—FOUR ROADS TO WINDRUSH
730—THE STARS OF SAN CECILIO
765—A CASE OF HEART TROUBLE
779—MISTRESS OF BROWN FURROWS
792—GATES AT DAWN
831—HOTEL AT TRELOAN
904—MOON AT THE FULL
926—MOUNTAIN MAGIC
967—THE WINGS OF THE MORNING
997—CASTLE THUNDERBIRD
1020—NO JUST CAUSE
1043—MARRY A STRANGER
1078—ROYAL PURPLE
1099—CARPET OF DREAMS
1128—THE QUIET HEART
1168—ROSE IN THE BUD
1189—ACCIDENTAL BRIDE
1221—MASTER OF MELINCOURT
1259—WILD SONATA
1311—THE MARRIAGE WHEEL
1359—RETURN TO TREMARTH
1428—NIGHT OF THE SINGING BIRDS
1526—BRIDE IN WAITING

Many of these titles are available at your local bookseller
or through the Harlequin Reader Service.

For a free catalogue listing all available Harlequin Romances,
send your name and address to:

HARLEQUIN READER SERVICE,
M.P.O. Box 707, Niagara Falls, N.Y. 14302
Canadian address: Stratford, Ontario, Canada N5A 6W2

or use coupon at back of book.

Victoria and the Nightingale

by

SUSAN BARRIE

Harlequin Books

TORONTO • LONDON • NEW YORK • AMSTERDAM
SYDNEY • HAMBURG • PARIS

Original hardcover edition published in 1967
by Mills & Boon Limited

ISBN 0-373-02240-9

Harlequin edition published February 1979

Printed in U.S.A.

CHAPTER ONE

IT WAS VERY DARK on the broad, straight stretch of road on which the accident had occurred. It was dark because as yet there was no moon, and as well as tall hedges there were towering trees shutting out the fields of shimmering grain and the patches of dense woodland receding into the dim distance on either side of the road.

Victoria prayed for the moon to rise, and wished she could do something about Johnny's shivering so very close to her side. She could actually hear the uncontrollable chattering of his teeth. The little girl who had remained absolutely tongue-tied throughout all the turmoil and the nightmare, and whose name she did not as yet know, kept such a tight hold of her hand that the small fingers had induced a feeling of numbness in her own, and try as she would she couldn't release them. She wanted to encircle the child with her arm, but that wasn't possible unless her hand was freed.

She spoke soothingly to both children, and in between trying to reassure them about the darkness, the silence, the continued absence of the police constable

who had gone to hunt for a phone booth and was trying to provide them with some means of transport,
made wild and desperate promises.

"It won't be long now," she said over and over
again. "The policeman will be back any minute now,
and there'll be a car to take us away from here.
You'll soon be cozily tucked up in bed, both of you,
with glasses of nice hot milk!"

She recollected that when she was young she had
disliked hot milk, but perhaps these two pathetic
creatures had a weakness for it. And, in any case, she
didn't really believe what she was saying.... For first
of all, beds had to be found for the children, and that
would mean further delays... police inquiries, possibly some sort of door-to-door search for people who
would take them in. There might be a hotel open that
would receive them, and she herself could put up
anywhere, even the local police station if there was
nowhere else.

But the children must have proper attention, and
that as promptly as possible. And more than anything else they required an understanding person to
take charge of them, and cope with the shock that
had numbed them temporarily.

She could make herself responsible for Johnny.
She had enough money to pay for hotel accommoda-
tion for both of them. But he was badly shocked...
stunned. He needed hospital treatment. And the
unknown little girl who was making dents in the palm
of her hand with her sharp nails needed careful
handling, also.

It was undoubtedly a case for a psychiatrist when these two small humans were capable of assimilating the fact that an accident had deprived them of their nearest and dearest.

In Johnny's case, at any rate, that was so. The little girl's parents had been badly hurt, but it was just possible they would live...or one of them might survive.

Victoria felt as if the nightmare returned as she pressed back against the hedge, and a wave of horror and nausea welled up over her. The children pressed closer to her. They were terrified of the road, the straight stretch of road on which terrifying scenes had taken shape before their eyes. And why they hadn't all been killed outright Victoria couldn't think.

The pileup of cars had been horrible. Johnny's father's...a neat convertible for which he was still paying, and behind the buckled wheel of which he had been pinned while she and Johnny had been flung clear. The car belonging to the parents of the little girl with fair hair who had lost the power of speech, had rolled over and over before it had made a violent noise like an explosion, and only the little girl had been miraculously unhurt on the back seat.

Johnny whispered:

"I'm c-cold...."

Victoria hugged him.

"You'll soon be warm." Again she was making wild promises. "There must be a town quite near."

The policeman's light came bobbing along the

road, but his face looked anxious when he reached them. He answered Victoria's unspoken query immediately.

"We'll be picked up in about half an hour. There just isn't a car available at the moment. It must be a night for accidents." He sank down on the grass verge beside her, and explained, "Another one over at High End, and Sergeant Buckley away on a course. It means that we've been caught off balance, as you might say, and we've all got to do double duty. But we will be picked up as soon as it can be managed. It's just a question of waiting."

He attempted to relieve Victoria of the little girl who clutched at her, but the child started screaming all at once, and she went on screaming so determinedly that he had to desist. Johnny was violently sick, and Victoria faced up to the indisputable fact that something had to be done about the situation immediately.

"Surely there's a house somewhere near at hand," she suggested to the policeman. "A cottage, at least?"

"There's only Wycherley Park."

"How far away is that?"

He indicated the dark woods behind them with his flashlight.

"It's back there in the trees. Sir Peter Wycherley's place. There are two lodges, but they're both approached from the other road, and the only way you can get to Wycherley Park is by taking a shortcut through the wood. I'd go myself, but I have my orders, and they're to stay put where we are now." Nevertheless, he looked as uncomfortable as a man with two small children of his own, who fully appreciated the desperate urgency of the situation and could do little or nothing about it, could possibly look under such circumstances. "It does seem a bit silly, I know, but orders are orders, and I can't go against them. However, it's pretty plain to me that the kids need help. That's a cut over the boy's eye, isn't it?" he asked, and he bent forward to inspect it.

"Yes, but it's not deep." In sheer desparation Victoria rose and at the same time managed to free her hand from the clasp of the little girl. "Why can't I go?" she suggested. "If you'll lend me your flashlight, I'm sure I can find my way."

The policeman looked startled.

"But those woods are deep. There's no proper track...."

"It doesn't matter. If you'll indicate the general direction of the house I can follow what track there is. I'm country born and bred, I won't get into difficulties."

"But on your own—"

"Why, are there poachers?"

The police constable looked indignant.

"We do our best to keep them down," he protested.

Victoria looked impatient.

"In any case, it doesn't really matter now, does it?" she said. "I've got to find this house."

She received the most concise instructions he could give her as to how to find it, and then she tried to hand Johnny over to his care, but Johnny was the one who now attached himself to her like a limpet. He refused to let her set off without him, and by this time the little girl had fallen into a kind of half-doze, and it was comparatively easy to transfer her to the doubtful comfort of the policeman's navy blue lap.

He sat cross-legged on the grass verge in the light of the slowly rising moon and hugged her to him a little awkwardly, while her fair hair streamed over his arm, and her small, pale, unconscious face upturned itself to the sky; and he warned Victoria to be as careful as she knew how, and if her effort to penetrate the wood proved too difficult, to come back. He also stated somewhat glumly that if he was severely reprimanded for allowing her to set off on her own— or what was even worse, hampered by Johnny—he would expect her to speak up for him to the superintendent when the opportunity came her way.

Victoria promised that she would do that very thing if it ever became necessary, and then possessed herself of his flashlight and set off.

At first the going was comparatively easy, for the path through the wood was fairly clear. And then it more or less petered out, and not even the fitful moon finding its way through the spreading branches above their heads helped matters. Johnny stumbled constantly, and all the time he whimpered and appealed to her like a lost soul, and she wished she had the strength to pick him up and carry him in her arms for the remainder of the way. But as he was a fairly well-developed little boy of eight years old she didn't think she could possibly manage this, and in any case the attempt might have precipitated them both into the underbrush... and as it was she was being badly scratched and scarred by the latter.

At last, miraculously, there was a clearing, and then the dark bulk of a house. But it was still surrounded by shrubberies, and the trees seemed to close in on it from the rear.

To the accompaniment of owls hooting in a melancholy manner in the depths of the wood behind them, and the occasional faraway bark of a fox, they made their way through a series of paddocks and orchards and a walled kitchen garden to another door in another high wall, and on the other side of that wall a well-cared-for drive swept like a snake around an angle of the house. And from the front of the house, when they reached it at last, lights were streaming forth and the unexpected brilliance illuminated the whole of the first sweep of the main drive.

Under normal circumstances Victoria would have been very much impressed by the tall Corinthian pillars that guarded the front door. She would have recognized that this was a very old house probably added to and extended about the beginning of the nineteenth century, and that inside it was almost certainly capacious and judging by the front of it in the flood of light in extremely good order. She had an impression of creeper-clad walls that received a lot of attention in order that the brickwork should sustain little or no damage, and the centuries-old lawns as smooth as billiard tables that crept close to the house, and dark cedar trees bending to inspect the turf. And although by this time he was in a very bad plight, Johnny was impressed—and also repelled—by the row of gleaming cars parked in the driveway.

He shrank nearer to Victoria, and was all for turning and bolting back into the shadows, only she prevented him. She whispered to him that it was perfectly all right, and he would soon be in bed.... And then determinedly she approached the front door.

She had already made up her mind that whoever owned the house—and apparently it was a Sir Peter Wycherley—he should put an end to Johnny's purely physical miseries. Johnny should have the very maximum amount of attention. That much she would insist on, despite the fact that she was not exactly in a condition to insist upon anything.

CHAPTER TWO

THE BUTLER WHO OPENED THE DOOR had a very surprised expression on his face. And the surprise grew as he took in the astonishing details of the pair who stood grouped on the doorstep.

The girl's corn-gold hair was wild and disheveled, and her face was chalk white. The boy was on the very point of collapse, and his clothing was stained with blood. Without waiting to ask any questions, since he was a man of action when he was not performing his more ponderous duties as a majordomo, the butler picked the child up in his arms and bore him into the very center of the hall, where the white light from a powerful crystal chandelier shone down upon them.

"There's been an accident, I suppose?" the butler said, looking over his shoulder at Victoria. "Where was it?"

She explained in a thin voice, "On the main road."

"The main road?" He could hardly believe her. "Then how did you get here? How in the name of—"

"Please." Her voice was thinner than ever. The white walls and the portraits and the graceful curving

staircase with its rose red carpet that flowed upward
into a gallery were proceeding to spin around her in a
strange, revolving corkscrewlike manner, and the
white light from the chandelier was positively blind-
ing her after the infinite darkness of the woods.
"Please, does it matter? I'd like to sit down...."

She groped her way to a chair, and the butler stood
holding Johnny and looking down at her as if this
really was something rather more than he could cope
with; and he didn't quite know whether to relinquish
Johnny and go to her assistance, or continue on his
way to the library, which had been his original
intention.

"I'll have to get help," he said, looking around
him helplessly. "But the housekeeper's gone to bed,
and the maids are off duty...." Voices reached
them—it seemed to Victoria that they were a tremendous way off—and laughter, and music that was
muffled by closed doors. Both the voices and the
music were light and bright, and a trifle hilarious, as
if the party was taking place out of sight, and had
gotten a little out of hand. "This isn't a good night,
I'm afraid. There are a lot of people here."

"People?"

"Guests. There was a dinner party, and since then
it's been going on for hours."

"Hours?" she whispered. "Then what time is
it?"

"It's three in the morning."

Victoria couldn't believe it. But then she was only

barely conscious, and she was beginning to be quite uncertain how that came about.

In the end, without disturbing the party—which apparently he hesitated to do—the butler lowered Johnny to a rug and went off to fetch cushions, brandy and a medical kit. He did his best with the medical kit while Johnny lay on the rug and Victoria slowly sipped the spirit that began by degrees to combat her overpowering sensation of faintness. Then he succeeded in arousing the housekeeper, and also one of the maids, who bore Johnny between them up the stairs to a guest room where they put him to bed and provided him with the hot milk and the comfort Victoria had promised him. All the while, Victoria sat in the hall and the butler telephoned for the local doctor, although Victoria protested that it wasn't necessary, and the sounds of music continued on the far side of the hall, and also the bursts of laughter.

"I think you'd be better off in the library, miss," the butler said, when he had made her some hot, strong tea and appeared with it on a tray. "Sir Peter isn't using it at the moment, and he won't mind if you rest there. When the doctor's been we'll know what to do with you."

"I'd much rather you went and fetched the little girl," Victoria objected, feeling this was all wrong. Perhaps she ought to go back and fetch the little girl, and relieve the anxiety of the policeman.

"Don't you worry, miss." The butler was horrified by the purple smudges under her eyes, and by the

evident strain and shock in the dark blue eyes themselves. And although she wasn't aware of it herself a
livid bruise was beginning to disfigure the area above
one of her cheekbones. "The doctor says the little
girl's been picked up by a police car and is on her way
to the hospital. She'll be well looked after when she
gets there. You don't have to worry."

He helped her into the library, and saw her comfortably installed in a deep leather armchair. He
placed the tray of tea beside her on a low occasional
table, and then although it was June he switched on a
powerful electric fire and finally left her to her own
devices while he went off to discuss the matter with
the housekeeper and decide whether or not they
ought to inform Sir Peter.

Victoria closed her eyes and fought against returning nausea. Try as she would she couldn't shut the horror of the accident out of her mental vision, and every
time it recurred she felt swamped by the nightmare of
it, and she wanted to run away somewhere where it
couldn't possibly pursue her. It was like falling into
uneasy dozes and dreaming horrifying dreams.

She was so thankful that Johnny was upstairs
somewhere in this great house, and that he was safely
tucked up in bed with a kindly Scottish housekeeper
to attend to him, and an equally kindly maidservant
to make a fuss over him.

Poor Johnny.... It was what he wanted...endless
fussing and cosseting, and no harsh awakening to
realities on the morrow.

For she was horribly afraid that on the morrow
Johnny would learn that he no longer had a parent.

It was very quiet in the library, and no intrusive
noises shattered the utter peace and tranquillity of it.
She opened her eyes and, in the one subdued light
that the butler had left burning, as well as the glow
from the electric fire, she could see the glass-fronted
bookshelves and the beautiful bindings they pro-
tected, the chrome leather of the chairs and the
deeper chrome of the carpet, the French windows
standing open to what remained of the night.

In an hour or so now the cocks would be crowing,
and the light of dawn would appear in the sky.
Already she thought she could detect a faint lighten-
ing of the sky toward the east, and there was that
breathless hush that precedes the dawn. The air was
cool, and there was the moist scent of roses floating
in through the French windows. Far, far away, or so
it seemed, a stable clock chimed the hour, and grandfather clocks all over the house joined in in a musical
medley.

Victoria felt herself drifting off into another one of
those uneasy—even terrifying—dozes, and she tried
to force herself to keep awake. She must have partially succeeded, for when she opened her eyes again
the stable chimes were still quivering in the atmosphere, and two people had come in through the
French window and were standing looking down at
her in astonishment.

"How extraordinary," a woman with a brittle,

amused voice exclaimed. "You don't think we're see-ing things, do you, darling? I mean—you were rather generous with the champagne tonight."

"Don't be silly." The man spoke sharply. "This young woman isn't a figment of our imagination. She appears to be taking a rest here."

"And she looks as if she might be the family ghost. She's awfully pale."

"And she's obviously in some sort of trouble." He coughed. "Excuse me—"

Victoria sat up with a jolt and grasped at the arms of the chair. If someone had presented her with a mirror just then she would have understood why they both continued to stare so hard.

"You are real, aren't you?" Even he sounded doubtful.

"Of course."

"Then you must have found your way in through the window. Are you looking for someone? Do you want something?"

She shook her head.

"Only to hear how Johnny is. And I think the doc-tor will be here any moment...."

But at that moment the door opened, and in came the doctor. He was a middle-aged man who had been in bed when he was sent for, and he wore his pajamas beneath an overcoat. He was accompanied by the housekeeper in a thick wool dressing gown, and the butler who was still in his formal black coat and pin-striped trousers. At sight of the two people who were standing staring at Victoria he looked mildly surprised, and then hurriedly explained.

"There's been an accident, Sir Peter. This young person was involved in it, and there's a child upstairs who has been put to bed by Mrs. Grainge and at the moment seems to be settling down quite comfortably. I thought the doctor ought to take a look at this young woman first—"

"You were quite right." The doctor ignored the rest of them and moved forward to the side of the chair that contained Victoria and bent over her. He smiled at her reassuringly as he picked up her wrist and felt her pulse. "You've had a nasty shock," he said. And then, over his shoulder, "I'd be glad if you would all leave the room while I make my examination...all, that is, except Mrs. Grainge, whom I shall probably need."

The butler looked mildly scandalized at the very idea of Sir Peter being requested to leave his own library, but Wycherley took the young woman with whom he had entered the room by the arm and propelled her toward the door.

"Out, sweetheart," he said. "We're not needed here."

She protested immediately, looking up at him with great dark eyes. She was a graceful slip of a thing in scarlet brocade, and not only was she attractive, but the depth and color of her dress emphasized her peculiarly exotic type of loveliness.

"But, Peter," she argued, "you can't have your

house turned into a kind of hospital just because
there's been an accident. We're having a celebration,
remember? And there's the local hospital. . . ."

"Probably they're full up," he replied, still urging
her purposefully toward the door. "And Dr. Brown
wants us out of here."

"But what about all the guests? You're not going
to break up the party?"

"It'll soon be breakfast time," he said, fairly
whisking her into the hall, "and it's high time the
party was broken up in any case."

As soon as they were outside, and the room was
cleared, the doctor gave his undivided attention to
Victoria. He pronounced, at last, that apart from a
few abrasions and some rather bad bruises she appeared to have sustained little damage—which was,
of course, remarkable; and at the moment she was
suffering from shock. He could tell by her dilated
eyes, and by the quality of her pallor, that she was
suffering from rather serious shock, and his pre-
scription was bed immediately, and on the following
day he would look in and give her a rather more
detailed examination just to make absolutely certain
there were no bones broken, or anything of that
sort.

He gave her an anti-tetanus injection, which made
her feel slightly worse than she had before, and then
he took the housekeeper aside and issued a few instructions. Victoria, who realized she was putting
these people to an enormous amount of trouble, and

perhaps it wasn't necessary if she could be fixed up
with a hotel room, or the local hospital would take
her in for the remainder of the night, interrupted the
discussion to protest feebly that she was perfectly all
right now, and she didn't think she ought to remain.
But the doctor crossed over to her again and smiled
at her understandingly.

"Don't be silly," he said. "You're not putting
anyone to undue trouble, and this house is so full of
rooms that are only infrequently used. Isn't that so,
Mrs. Grainge?" He appealed to the housekeeper.

She was a motherly woman with a Scottish accent,
and she answered at once.

"That's right, love." She laid a hand on Victoria's
shoulder. "And Sir Peter's a very kind gentleman
and you mustn't take any notice of what Miss Islesworth said because she's only become engaged to Sir
Peter, and tonight they were having a bit of a celebration...an engagement party I suppose you'd call
it."

"Oh, I'm sorry." Victoria was sorry, and she
looked faintly appalled.

Mrs. Grainge patted her gently on the shoulder.

"It's not your fault, love. Accidents will happen,
and the little lad upstairs is the one to be sympathized
with if his father was badly injured in the crash. Let's
hope there'll be some good news of him tomorrow."
She looked rather more curiously at Victoria. "Is the
gentleman a relative of yours, my dear?"

Victoria answered briefly, "My employer."

"I see."

The doctor looked impatient at this questioning, and Mrs. Grainge recollected what was expected of her. She withdrew to supervise the preparation of a bedroom for Victoria, and Dr. Brown took his leave after once more feeling the victim's pulse and explaining that he had left a sedative for her to take, and that he would look in and see her early the following morning. He then made his way upstairs to have a look at Johnny.

Victoria was once more alone when Sir Peter came back into the library and stood regarding her with a good deal of quite unconcealed concern in his eyes.

They were very pleasant—even exceptionally attractive—gray eyes, and for a man his eyelashes were unusually long and thick and dark. He was a slenderly built man a little above average height, and he had light brown hair and well-cut features, and a slight air of diffidence seemed to cling to him, although under normal circumstances his lips could curve humorously and there was often a humorous twinkle in his eyes. It was quite obvious that he had an excellent tailor, for his evening clothes were beautifully cut and fitted him to perfection, and the impeccable quality of his linen threw into prominence the rather dark cast of his countenance.

Either he had lived abroad a good deal, and acquired a healthy tan, or his light brown hair should have been dark as a raven's wing to suit the bronze of his skin and the strange blackness of his lashes.

When he smiled at Victoria she felt strangely warmed and comforted by his smile. She certainly didn't feel that he regarded her as a nuisance, even if his recently acquired fiancée thought of her as such.

"How are you feeling?" he asked, as she lay somewhat limply in the chair and he stood beside it and looked down at her. "I'm afraid you've had rather a nasty time. Was that needle of old Brown's very painful when he gave you the injection?"

She shook her head, and for a moment she felt too vague to answer him. Then she managed a rather husky whisper.

"It didn't hurt at all. But I'm feeling a bit confused. It all happened so suddenly," she said in a more throaty whisper.

"I understand." He moved nearer to her, and for one moment she thought he was going to rest his hand on her shoulder as his housekeeper had done. "I've been up to look at the child, but I don't think you have to worry about him too much. Children have a way of surviving these things better than adults."

She agreed with him that this was miraculously so.

"I understand his father is—in pretty poor shape. . . ."

She nodded and agreed with him, this time soundlessly.

"I telephoned the hospital. The report is not good. But of course it may be better tomorrow."

She made a faint movement with her lips. For the

first time she realized that he was studying her hand—her left hand, which was completely ringless.

"The child is not yours?" he stated rather than asked.

Her drugged blue eyes—and they were as deep and dark as harebells—expressed surprise.

"No."

"But he is some sort of a relative?"

"No."

Sir Peter Wycherley moved awkwardly. Perhaps he realized that this was no time for questioning.

"My—my fiancée was a little upset just now," he murmured. "You mustn't think she objects to your presence in the house. As a matter of fact, she's intensely sympathetic, and would like to provide you with everything you need during your stay here. Fortunately she, too, is staying here, and she has plenty of things with her." He made a vague gesture with his hand. "Sleeping things and so on. She's put everything you'll require in your room."

"That—that's extraordinarily kind of her," Victoria murmured back, and then struggled to her feet because she thought that if she didn't reach her room soon she might disgrace herself by being sick, or fainting, or something of the sort. She stood literally swaying on her feet and added: "In fact, you're both very kind. You're all being very—very—very k-ki—"

And then her senses deserted her quite abruptly, and Sir Peter caught her in his arms before she fell and narrowly averted a further catastrophe as a result of her head hitting the stone hearth and possibly causing concussion. He held her for a moment as if she were a baby in his arms, and he thought how exceptionally fair her hair was, and how thin and pinched her face.

Then without any further hesitation he bore her out into the hall and up his gracious curving staircase to the room that had been prepared for her.

CHAPTER THREE

VICTORIA FELT CONFUSED the following morning when she awakened in a completely strange room with morning sunlight finding its way into it round the edges of the drawn curtains.

She lay in the pleasant twilight that filled the greater part of the room and tried to think up some convincing explanation of the reason why she was where she was, and the explanation had to include such trifling reassurances as a satisfactory excuse for her wearing a nightdress that most certainly didn't belong to her; and for all the solid comfort and luxury that surrounded her.

She was used to reasonable comfort in her surroundings, but this was comfort run riot. Facing her was a splendid tallboy with a degree of polish that made her blink, and over in the wide window space was the kind of dressing table she had often dreamed of possessing one day but never seriously hoped to do. It stood in a petticoat of flowered satin and had an oval mirror that appeared to be framed in beaten silver standing on it, and there were a lot of silver-topped bottles and some crystal flagons and things scattered about the plate-glass surface as well.

She could see a vast wardrobe, and that, too, was shimmering as if housemaids worked on it constantly, and what she decided was a tall pier-glass or cheval mirror, and a long couch covered in the same flowered satin as that which provided a skirt for the dressing table. And there appeared to be a vast area of carpet, and it was rosily pink like a cloud; and some rugs that were white clouds floating on the pink cloud.

She frowned as she lay looking at it all and decided that this was no hotel room. Johnny's father couldn't possibly afford a room like this.... And then all at once she remembered, and with memory surging back her head began to ache.

Mrs. Grainge came quietly into the room with a tray of tea, and the first thing she did was draw the curtains, then she approached the bed and smiled at the occupant.

"Well," she said, "and how did you sleep? You're looking better, I must say."

Victoria felt horribly confused still, but at least she knew now what it was all about.

"Johnny—" she asked, and the housekeeper poured her a cup of tea and smiled even more complacently.

"Doing nicely," she assured her. "As bright as a button this morning, although a bit worried because you're not around. Apparently you look after him, and he seems to think you're his special property."

"I—I do look after him," Victoria admitted.

The housekeeper poised the sugar tongs above the sugar bowl.

"Two lumps, dear?" she asked.

Victoria nodded.

"A kind of nursery governess, is that it, dear?" the housekeeper pursued. "I'd say he's a bit old to need a nanny."

"Oh, it's nothing like that...." Victoria, despite the dull ache in her head, felt she ought to explain. "You see, I used to do welfare work, and I worked with children, and Johnny's father was a widower, and needed someone to cook and look after Johnny. He was—he is," she corrected herself for some reason that she didn't quite understand—"a door-to-door salesman, and he doesn't have much time to look after Johnny himself. The welfare people thought it would be a good thing for me to help him out, so I did...I mean, I went and lived in and took charge of Johnny. We—we're having a bit of a holiday now...."

"I see," but the housekeeper didn't sound as if she entirely understood.

Victoria was groping her way through the confusion that clouded her brain.

"How—how is he?" she asked huskily, remembering.

Mrs. Grainge went across to the dressing table and started busying herself by altering the position of one of the cut-glass perfume bottles, and lifting the heavy silver-backed hand mirror from the tray. She replaced it after a moment, during which she had had time to make up her mind.

"I don't think Sir Peter has had any news from the hospital yet," she said. "But he'll tell you all about it when he does."

She returned briskly to the bedside.

"Now, what would you like for breakfast?" she asked, the smooth and amiable mask on her face again. "I'm not going to let you get up yet, because I think you need a rest, and Dr. Brown wanted you to stay in bed until he'd seen you again. But I do think you need a good breakfast. What about scrambled eggs and some grapefruit beforehand? And coffee? Or would you prefer tea?"

"Tea, please." But Victoria struggled up on her pillows and felt certain that she ought to get up at once and satisfy herself about Johnny's condition. After all, he was surrounded by strangers, and he was not the type to make friends easily. "I ought to see Johnny—"

"After breakfast, if the doctor allows it." Mrs. Grainge was quite firm, but she smiled pleasantly. "You must think of yourself as well as the child, you know."

"But he's had a dreadful shock, and I'm the only one he knows. I ought to be with him."

"You can safely leave him to us. And believe me, he's not at all unhappy." Mrs. Grainge unhooked a dressing gown from off the door, and laid it across the foot of the bed in readiness for Victoria to slip into. "Miss Islesworth lent you this, and there are a lot of other things belonging to her in the wardrobe that you can wear if you want to. I'm afraid your own clothes are in a very bad condition." For the first time that morning she looked at the girl in the bed with real sympathy in her eyes. "That was a dreadful accident you were involved in, and there's a lot of blood and oil on your things."

"Blood and oil?" Victoria began to feel faint again. "But Johnny and I were practically un-hurt...."

Mrs. Grainge spoke quickly.

"There, there, perhaps I shouldn't have mentioned it! And in any case, we can't be absolutely certain that it's blood. It could be marks from the road." She was startled by the expression in Victoria's eyes, and she hurried out of the room. "I'll get your break-fast," she muttered as she went.

As soon as she was alone Victoria made a supreme effort and eased herself out of bed. Every bone in her body felt like an aching tooth, and she felt a little dizzy when she stood up. But her head was compara-tively clear again.

She slipped into the dressing gown, and it was the first time in her life that she had donned anything so luxurious so early in the morning. It was a white silk sheath, and when it was fastened round her she real-ized that the fit was perfect. She and Miss Islesworth must be almost the same build.

She opened the door of the wardrobe and saw the clothes that had been put there for her. They, too, were unlike anything she had ever worn before. Under normal circumstances she would have been thrilled by the thought of wearing them. But now she was consumed by the urgent desire to dress and face the world, and she wasn't at all sure how she was going to manage on her own.

She moved slowly and painfully across the thick carpet until she stood in front of the dressing table, and she looked at herself in the mirror. Her reflection startled her. She had no color at all, and her eyes looked enormous. Normally they were blue—a dreamy, delightful blue; but with distended pupils and darkened irises they could have been black.

Her small, heart-shaped face looked wan and pinched, and the livid bruise over her left cheekbone was acquiring some frightening hues. As for her hair—and she was proud of her soft, spun-silk, corn-gold hair—she had never seen it look so drab, and there were one or two burrs adhering to it that she had collected on her passage through the wood the night before.

She picked them out with unsteady fingers, and then decided that before she could eat she must have a bath. And she was actually in her bath when Mrs. Grainge returned with her breakfast tray.

The bathroom adjoined the bedroom, and the housekeeper waited with the white silk robe in her hands until she was ready to slip into it again. She

shook her head at her and clucked at her as she sat
down at last behind the breakfast tray, but even then
she wasn't really surprised when Victoria looked with
horror at the scrambled egg, although she greedily
drank three cups of tea.

The doctor arrived before Victoria had had a
chance to dress, and after one long and careful look
at her he insisted that she go straight back to bed.
Under the influence of more sedatives she slept for
the greater part of that day, and the next morning she
woke feeling almost like herself, and was horrified
because she had allowed herself to lie drugged and
supine while Johnny was in another part of the house
and possibly needing her.

But before the doctor called that morning Johnny
himself arrived in her room, looking so normal that
she experienced a tremendous surge of gratitude for
his normality.

He climbed on to her bed in a freshly washed and
mended T-shirt, and the short shorts that he had been
wearing at the time of the accident, and told her that
he had been having a wonderful time in the charge of
one of the under-house maids, and the big bedroom
in which he was sleeping was full of toys and books
and everything that could possibly delight his heart.
Victoria later discovered that it was part of the at
present unused nursery quarters of the house, and
many of the boxes of soldiers and the toy forts and
train sets had been played with by Sir Peter Wycherley when he was young.

Victoria and Johnny breakfasted together on that second morning of their stay at Wycherley Park, and afterward the doctor came and looked at them both again, and Victoria was permitted to get up. She dressed herself in a selection of the garments Miss Islesworth had so generously made over to her, and afterward she consigned Johnny to the care of the under-housemaid once more and made her way downstairs to the library.

Sir Peter had sent up a message to the effect that, if she felt up to it, he would see her in the library; and perhaps because she had suddenly become hypersensitive and, indeed, a trifle clairvoyant, she knew before she reached the library that he had unpleasant tidings to convey to her.

From Mrs. Grainge she had learned nothing about Johnny's father, or the fate of the other victims of the accident. Dr. Brown had refused to discuss the subject with her, and now it was left to Sir Peter to put her in possession of some highly disturbing facts.

She was so sure of this that she stopped outside the library door when she reached it, having been directed to it by no less a person than Forster, the butler, himself, and drew a deep breath—a very deep breath—before knocking hesitantly on the panels of the door and waiting for a voice to call out to her to enter.

But Sir Peter didn't call out to her to enter. He whipped open the door himself, and stood looking at her with a mixture of conflicting expressions on his face as he indicated the chair she had occupied when she first entered the library.

"You are feeling better?" She was wearing a slim little dress in navy and white, and it was deceptively simple and smelled delicately of exclusive French perfume. He made the same observation that the housekeeper had made. "You are certainly looking better."

Victoria answered in a small, awkward voice, by no means certain how she looked the night she demanded sanctuary in his home, but more or less convinced that she must have looked frightful.

"I—I'm feeling very much better, thank you."

"And rested?"

She smiled somewhat twistedly.

"I should be. I spent the whole of yesterday in bed, and I didn't get up for breakfast this morning. I'm developing lazy habits."

Having seen her comfortably installed in the chair Sir Peter went round the room touching books and papers in an obviously embarrassed and quite definitely constrained manner. He was not the aggressive country gentleman in his well-cut tweeds, but he did look the part he was called upon to play, and he did look as if it was natural to him to behave as a courteous and considerate host, and her suggestion that she was developing lazy habits appeared to surprise him.

"Why, do you never breakfast in bed?" he asked.

"Only when I'm ill, or threatening to be ill."

"Then you certainly had an excuse for remaining

in bed yesterday." His eyes narrowed as he gazed at her. "I didn't come near you or disturb you because I thought you would prefer to be undisturbed."

"Thank you, Sir Peter," she answered automatically.

"I understand your name is Wood—Miss Victoria Wood—and that you are an employee of one of the—one of the victims of the accident."

"That's right." She swallowed, because there was a sudden tension in the atmosphere, and she more or less prepared herself for what was coming next. He was still fidgeting with various papers on his desk, but she saw him abandon them suddenly and—only pausing to light himself a cigarette, as if he felt he might need it—he came toward her. "That's right," she repeated, swallowing again. "I am employed by Johnny's father to look after Johnny. Is he—is he—"

She could go no further.

"The child upstairs seems perfectly well." He deliberately misunderstood her to give himself time.

"I know. I've seen him. But his—father...?"

"I'm sorry, Miss Wood, but your employer is dead."

Victoria sat staring at the handsome specimen of a wide baronial fireplace that was one of the important features of the library, and for several seconds she could say nothing. She had steeled herself to hear this, but now that she had heard it she was frankly appalled.

Johnny...? What would happen to Johnny? His father would have left behind him nothing but debts—he had been coping with difficult times, she knew—and there were no near relatives to come forward and claim the child. So far as she knew there were not any relatives at all, and hardly any friends. The little house in a London suburb where they had lived had been visited infrequently by outsiders, and apart from his school friends Johnny had appeared to know literally no one.

It was not really surprising that, when she first knew him, he had seemed a strange, withdrawn, slightly morbid child who concentrated on morbid subjects...and when he brought in a dead robin from the garden he wanted to keep it in a box because he had fed it when it was alive, and he looked upon it as his particular property. He had so little of his own that he did not wish to lose the robin.

"I . . . ." She drew a deep breath. "Johnny doesn't know yet, of course?"

"No."

"You think I should be the one to tell him?"

"I think he'll probably take it better from you."

That rather alarming feeling of faintness began to creep over her again, and Sir Peter realized it and went to a corner cupboard and produced a bottle of brandy. He poured her a small glassful and held it out to her.

"Drink this," he said. "I think you need it."

Her teeth rattled against the glass.

"The other night was the first time I tasted brandy," she admitted, feeling her breath catch in her throat as she gulped at it somewhat too hurriedly.

"That doesn't mean you're going to become an addict from now on." There was a faint but very human smile on his lips as he helped to steady the glass. "Quite the contrary! You'll probably hate the sight and smell of it because it will remind you of this rather difficult phase of your life."

She lifted her strained dark blue eyes to his, and she saw that his gray ones were watching her gravely.

"I'd better hear the rest of it, Sir Peter," she whispered. "What happened to the others? The little girl and her parents?"

"The little girl is still slightly shocked, but she's recovering in hospital," he answered. "As a matter of fact, I went to see her yesterday."

"You did?"

"Yes." He moved away, and flicked ash into the grate. "Such a poor, pathetic mite of a thing!" His gray eyes darkened. "But she's better off than Johnny, because both her parents survived, and one of them's making quite good progress. An aunt has come forward to take the child, and she'll make herself responsible for her until one or both parents are discharged from hospital and in a fit condition to have the little girl again."

"Oh, I'm so glad." Victoria drew a long, shuddering breath of relief. Looking back on the whole dark episode she realized that fate must have been intervening on Johnny's behalf when he insisted on accompanying her through the wood instead of remaining with the policeman, because now, at least, he was still with her, and he had been provided with a purely temporary home.

But just how temporary was that home likely to be? Almost certainly very temporary!

She decided it was her duty to broach the subject.

"With regard to—Johnny," she said, "something will have to be decided about his future, and very soon. He can't stay here."

Sir Peter looked thoughtful.

"I've been thinking about that," he admitted, starting to pace up and down the room. "It is a bit of a problem, I admit."

"But not your problem, Sir Peter," understanding perfectly what he meant.

He looked surprised.

"I don't quite follow you. The child has survived a very bad accident, and the effects are likely to develop later even if there is little sign of them at present. And he doesn't, of course, know about his father. He will have to remain here, of course, until something is settled about him."

A tremendous feeling of relief assailed Victoria.

"You're very kind," she said. "Johnny would thank you if he understood how badly you are upsetting your household in order to provide him with a temporary refuge."

Sir Peter continued his pacing up and down, but

one of his eyebrows seemed more or less permanently raised.

"Don't be silly, Miss Wood," he said a little short-ly. "My household is not being upset by Johnny, and the house itself is big enough to provide him with what you call refuge without anyone who didn't want to becoming involved in the child's concerns. I myself have seen little of him since he has been here, and my staff take their orders from me. Quite apart from which they seem to have taken a fancy to Johnny himself, and are, of course, extremely sorry for him and his orphaned condition."

"I was thinking of Miss Islesworth," Victoria ad-mitted, a trifle huskily.

Sir Peter stood still and looked at her. Then he nodded.

"Yes, there is that. But Miss Islesworth is perfectly human, you know, and so far as I am aware she has no objections to Johnny being the recipient of my hospitality."

"Miss Islesworth has been very kind," Victoria said, in the same husky voice. "She lent me this dress," touching it, "as well as a lot of other things. I would like you please to convey to her my appreciation."

The man in front of her appeared surprised.

"You can do that yourself, can't you, when you see her?" he suggested.

Victoria rose up out of her chair. All at once she felt extremely agitated because something had to be settled, and the sooner it was settled the better.

"But, Sir Peter," she objected, "you know I can't stay on here until someone comes forward to take charge of Johnny." Her small, peaked face looked desperately anxious and desperately worried. "It's my job to look after him—or rather, it was." She swallowed. "But now that Johnny's father is dead the position is entirely changed. I haven't any right to stay here with him."

"You mean," with unexpected coldness, "that with Johnny's father dead you are unlikely to receive anything in the nature of a salary?"

Victoria was appalled because he could even make such a suggestion.

"S-salary?" she stammered. And then she smiled wanly. "Poor Mr. Musgrove, Johnny's father, was always so hard up that I don't think I've received any salary for several weeks. I'm afraid he didn't earn very much, and he was an inveterate gambler, so, apart from the housekeeping money he gave me—when he could manage it—there was never anything over. I didn't mind," hurriedly, in case once again he should get the wrong impression, "because I've grown so attached to Johnny, and I've a small sum in the bank that enabled me to buy my personal things."

This time Sir Peter was astounded, and he also looked perplexed.

"You mean," he said, "that you've been working for nothing for Johnny's father?"

"For a few months, yes."

"What sort of a position did you occupy in his household?"

Victoria smiled at the grandiose term.

"I was his housekeeper. And I looked after Johnny."

Sir Peter helped himself to another cigarette somewhat hurriedly, lit it, cast it away and lit another before he commented.

"Forgive me," he said at last, "but aren't you a little young to act the part of housekeeper to a man of Johnny's father's age? A widower, I understood!"

She understood the implication, and flushed. It was the first time since he had met her that he saw real color in her face.

"I expect it does seem a little odd to you," she remarked, "and I know I'm not very old. I'm twenty-two, as a matter of fact. But Johnny's father was in desperate need of someone to help out with Johnny, and the welfare center where I worked did their best to help him out. But he couldn't pay much, and—and—" She spread her hands awkwardly. "I wasn't in desperate need of being paid, and I've always loved Johnny. I had to go to their assistance, and the welfare people thought it was all right. But—you don't?" she added helplessly.

He shrugged.

"I didn't say so."

"No, but I'm sure you think the whole arrangement was...well, unconventional," flushing more brilliantly than ever.

He was surveying her curiously, and very directly.

"I gather that Johnny's father was quite a young man?"

"Y-yes."

"Was he thinking of marrying again?"

She gazed at him with widened eyes.

"You mean, was he thinking of marrying me?"

"Well, was he?"

"Certainly not!" she answered with emphasis. And then all at once her strained blue eyes darkened and sparkled ominously. "I see you can't accept that," she exclaimed in a rush of indignation. "To you it seems obvious that I was interested in Johnny's father as well as Johnny. Just because I was prepared to work without wages—we call them that in my world," as if she wanted to emphasize the difference in their positions—"to you it's quite obvious that there were other considerations that made the job worth having. But you're quite, quite wrong"—her slim breasts heaving—"you couldn't be more wrong! Poor Mr. Musgrove is dead, and I couldn't be more sorry because I liked him and I think he liked and approved of me, but beyond that our relationship had absolutely no highlights. I knew when I took the job that some people might think it strange, but that didn't matter, not to me! Mr. Musgrove adored his wife, and I know that he would never, never have considered marrying again.... And as for me—"

"Well?" Sir Peter waited. "As for you?"

"I don't even—like—men very much."

She saw him smile, and she knew that she had convinced him. But her long speech had exhausted her, and all at once she looked so shaken and exhausted that he conducted her personally back to her chair and put her into it.

"Now listen to me," he said.

CHAPTER FOUR

HE TOLD HER THAT he had decided to keep Johnny at Wycherley Park until some satisfactory arrangement for his future could be arrived at. The authorities were perfectly happy about this, and if she was prepared to stay and felt up to it he would like her to continue to have charge of him. She was used to Johnny, and the child needed her and quite plainly seemed to cling to her, and unless she wished to leave immediately and rejoin her own parents—whom he felt should have been notified about the accident before this!—he hoped she would remain, at any rate until the ordeal of the funeral was over, and Johnny had had a chance to settle down.

"If you'll let me have the address of your parents I'll communicate with them," he said.

"I haven't any parents," she answered.

He didn't look particularly surprised.

"Then some close relative...?"

"I haven't any close relatives."

This time he looked faintly surprised.

"My father was a farmer, and he, too, was a widower for years," she explained, "and I never had any brothers or sisters. We lived in Hampshire, and our farm was razed to the ground by fire, and my father died in the fire. That was two years ago.'' She spoke jerkily, as if the memory still upset her. ''My father died trying to save his horses.''

Sir Peter looked really shocked.

''And did he?'' he asked.

She simply shook her head.

All at once he decided that this inquisition had gone far enough. He spoke decidedly, as if he had made up his mind for her.

''I take it that you still want to be with Johnny,'' he said, ''and that you're not prepared to desert him when he needs you most. So for the next fortnight or so, at least, shall we agree that you'll stay on here? Your clothes and things can be sent for, and we'll get you comfortably settled in. Anything you need you have but to ask for, and I think Forster and Mrs. Grainge have decided to move you into another wing of the house where you and Johnny can be together. It's the old nursery wing, and there, at least, you'll be entirely free to do as you please.'' He paused for a moment, and then said more thoughtfully, ''You're free, of course, to move about in any other part of the house if you wish to. And you can go wherever you like in the grounds.''

''Thank you,'' she said...a trifle inadequately, she realized.

''Someone will have to tell Johnny...about his father!'' he went on.

She looked absolutely aghast.

"Yes," she agreed, in a whisper.

"Do you feel up to it?"

"Not really." Her hands went cold at the very thought.

"Then you can leave it to me. Afterward he can come to you for comfort."

She looked at him with sudden tears of gratitude in her eyes.

"You're very good, very kind," she told him, barely audibly. "I...Johnny and I are both terribly grateful!"

"You don't have to feel grateful, and I'm neither good nor kind." For the first time his smile at her had a touch of sweetness and gentleness that shook her slightly. She had never met a man in the least like him before, and she had certainly never met one who was a baronet and human at the same time—apparently distinctly human.

But she still found herself wondering about Miss Islesworth.

She wondered, too, whether she was still staying in the house.

For the next few days she and Johnny were left very much to themselves—apart, that is, from the interest Mrs. Grainge and the butler took in them; but there was the one occasion when Sir Peter sent for Johnny and kept him closeted with him in the library for quite a long time, and afterward Johnny burst in on Victoria and showed her a pair of red-rimmed eyes, then rushed at her and dissolved into further tears while she kept him on her lap and rocked him in her arms like a baby.

From the moment he recovered his composure, however, he never again referred to the accident... or not for a very long time. But while he was still struggling to get the better of his misery he endeavored to get one or two minor matters straight.

"Does this mean we won't ever be going—home again?"

"No, darling, not to Cedar Avenue."

"Will we be living—here?"

"For a while, yes. But only for a while," she was careful to stress.

"And after that?"

"Arrangements will be made. But don't worry, sweetheart, they'll be quite nice arrangements," without any real conviction in her heart. "For you, at any rate," she added hurriedly.

Johnny looked at her in an alarmed fashion.

"But what about you? We will be together, won't we?" he insisted. He shook her arm in sudden frenzy. "Won't we?"

"I...I hope so, honey."

His enormous eyes raked her face.

"You're not quite certain?"

She realized that this was no time for letting him know the truth, and she had no idea what Sir Peter Wycherley had said to him, so she decided to be reckless and give him the reassurance that he so obviously craved. She hugged him in her arms and she said over and over again: "Yes, yes, darling, I'm sure we'll be together!" She prayed wildly that it would work out that way. "If that's what you want, we'll be together!"

Johnny looked up at her with eyes like solemn, moistly gleaming, red-rimmed lamps and assured her that he wanted nothing else.

"Just you and me," he said, "Just you and me!"

For no particular reason she heard herself asking him:

"But what about Sir Peter? Don't you like him?"

"Yes," he answered immediately, "I like him, and he's promised to buy me a lot more toys as well as those they've given me to play with now. And he talked to me about playing cricket and football one day, and said I could have a pony if I'd like one. And he's promised to show me the horses—the proper horses!" He looked temporarily diverted. "But," he added unexpectedly, "he's a man—he's not you!"

"You're a baby," she said, and sat crooning over him until teatime, when he was diverted once again by the sight of the chocolate cake that had been baked for him by the cook, and which occupied a prominent position in the center of the nursery tea table. And there were so many other delicacies besides that Victoria experienced a pang of uneasiness for the future, when there would be no nursery teas of this high quality, and no butler and housekeeper to take a particular interest in him and buy him presents with their own money...and no Sir Peter Wycherly to promise a pony, and gratify his other childish whims.

She managed to obtain permission from the hospital to visit the little girl who had attached herself to her like a limpet on the night of the accident, and she was pleased to see that she was bearing up remarkably well, and already the shock of the accident seemed to have lessened its effect.

Victoria was driven in to the hospital by Sir Peter's chauffeur in a long, gray car that had its backseat crowded to capacity with gifts from the staff at Wycherley Park, and in addition to those gifts she stopped the car in the local market town and bought sweets and books for the small patient she was visiting. She had no need to buy anything for Johnny, for he was snowed under with what he had already received.

The funeral of Johnny's father was a pathetic affair, the memory of which lingered for a long time in her mind. Once again a Wycherley Park car was placed at her disposal, and she was driven to the church where the interment took place by Sir Peter's chauffeur, whom she was beginning to know quite well by this time.

Sir Peter himself did not accompany her, possibly because he would have felt like an intruder at a time when there was really no room for intruders, and Johnny, of course, remained behind in the nursery. So there was no one, actually, to give Victoria support,

although when she left the churchyard she found
Mrs. Grainge waiting for her. The housekeeper explained that Sir Peter had thought that she ought to
have someone to return with her to the Park . . . someone in addition to the chauffeur who waited for her,
and who was separated from her by a glass screen
when they were actually on the road.

Victoria returned to Wycherley Park feeling far
older than her twenty-two years, and certainly
more experienced than a good many girls of her
age.

For the second time in less than three years she had
known shock and violence, and for the second time
she felt unutterably bereft. It wasn't because she had
been all that close to John Musgrove, who had failed
so often to pay her any wages; but, as a man—and
because of an unfortunate affair when she was only
nineteen, she really did mistrust, and was inclined to
dislike, all men—she had found him pleasant to work
for, and extremely appreciative even if he didn't
show his appreciation in any very practical way. And
more than anything else, he had been Johnny's
father, and Johnny, who adored him, was now the
apple of her eye.

Without Johnny she would indeed feel as if she
had been cast adrift on a strange ocean, without any
real hope of seeing land again. And without Johnny
she would have no one for whom she need feel responsible, no one who cared about her enough to
threaten floods of tears if he thought he was going to

be permanently separated from her, and no one—and this was the most important thing—to plan for.

If only she could go on planning for Johnny. If only it was the day-to-day planning of one who was engaged to look after him. A child of that age could not be planned for unless he really belonged to one, and Johnny, she knew, would never belong to her. If she had been married to his father he would belong to her. But there had never been one single, solitary moment when she had contemplated marrying Johnny's father.

Although, in all honesty, she had to admit to herself, Johnny's father had perturbed her somewhat a few weeks before by hinting that he might one day marry again, and further hinting that there was only one person in the world whom Johnny would welcome as stepmother.

It had been merely a hint—and a look—that had thrown her off balance for several days. And if it had been repeated she would have had to hand in her notice.

But it had not been repeated, and she was with Johnny when his father was killed.

When she returned from the funeral she went to her own room for a short while, and sat there thinking of what had taken place that afternoon, and how much it was going to mean to Johnny, before she went to join him in the nursery.

On her way to it she saw that a door of one of the major guest rooms was standing open, and a pile of luggage had been deposited in the middle of the floor by one of the housemaids. When the girl emerged into the corridor Victoria asked her who it was who had come to stay, and was not entirely surprised when the girl replied that it was Miss Islesworth.

Victoria didn't stop to ask any more questions, such as where was Miss Islesworth at that particular moment, but went on down the corridor to the nursery. She opened the door, as she normally did, rather briskly, and almost recoiled into the corridor when she saw that Johnny, instead of sitting waiting for her alone, as she had pictured him, had a visitor.

Georgina Islesworth was sitting in the lap of a deep chesterfield couch while Johnny sat on the floor and played with a train set. Miss Islesworth was wearing a fetching suit and hat, and she looked as if she had recently emerged from the hands of a beautician. She also looked extremely aristocratic and aloof, as befitted the granddaughter of an earl—albeit one whose family had recently been hit hard by death duties— and extremely thoughtful as she contemplated Johnny at the moment of Victoria's entry.

Instantly her expression, that had been coolly affable, froze. She rose and looked at Victoria as if she positively disliked her, although she knew little or nothing about her. And the fact that Victoria was wearing black shoes and gloves and an unpretentious gray suit that she had bought herself before the funeral did nothing to soften her expression.

"So you're back," she said. "I didn't know you

were coming back. I thought—" gesturing toward the child on the floor—"that one of the maids was going to look after him, and you were leaving. Hasn't it already struck you that it's asking rather a lot of Sir Peter Wycherley to maintain both you and the boy? I mean to say, as his fiancée I do feel that your return here is carrying things rather far, and even Peter, good-natured though he is, can't be imposed on forever! How soon do you leave?"

CHAPTER FIVE

VICTORIA FELT LIKE someone who had most unexpectedly had the ground cut from beneath her feet. She supposed, when she thought about it afterward, that she should have been prepared for this. She had heard Miss Islesworth express herself somewhat forcefully on the night of her and Johnny's arrival, but since then she had displayed a good deal of generosity in providing her, Victoria, with quite an outfit of clothes to wear since she had little or nothing of her own, and on the one or two occasions when they met she had been polite, if distant.

She had left Wycherley Park two days after the accident, but now, apparently, she had returned to stay for a long time, if the pile of luggage on the floor of her bedroom was anything to go by. And she was in a truculent mood, a mood to put this young woman who claimed sanctuary at Wycherley in her place. It should have occurred to Victoria that when a man becomes engaged to be married he should, by right, consult his fiancée about every important decision that he made once the engagement had been announced...and Sir Peter had merely seemed to take it for granted that the dark and devastating Georgina would be only too happy to support him in his decision to keep Johnny at Wycherley, at any rate for a time.

There was, of course, no question of Johnny remaining at the Park for good.

But it was now abundantly clear that Miss Islesworth had either not been consulted, or she was actively rebelling as a result of a certain amount of afterthought. In any case, she had a perfect right to object, as Victoria would have been the first to admit. And she swallowed something in her throat and apologized hastily for inflicting herself on Sir Peter.

"Of course, I do realize that he has been tremendously kind." She moistened her lips with her tongue, recalling vaguely that she had been dying for a cup of tea when she entered the nursery, and had been hoping in the same vague, curiously exhausted way that the nursery maid who looked after them would bring one to her as soon as she knew she was back. But now she couldn't have swallowed a glass of water if it was offered to her. Her throat felt dry and stiff. "No one could have been kinder than Sir Peter. . . to myself as well as Johnny!"

"No one is disputing that Johnny, as a child in desperate need, should stay here and be looked after," Miss Islesworth returned, with rather more reasonableness in her tone. She glanced at Johnny as if she, personally, was not attracted by him, but she was a humanist, and all children had to be cared for. "For a time, at least," she amended her statement. "Until some other arrangement can be made for him."

Victoria moistened her lips again.

"Of course not," she said, "There was never any intention that Johnny should stay here for good."

Georgina looked surprised, and her eyes flashed.

"I should hope not!" she declared. "Sir Peter is a bachelor, and when he's married he will not wish to start his married life hampered by someone else's child. Why, the very thought is outrageous!"

Johnny plainly disliked her tone, for he left his train set and crept across the floor to Victoria. He caught at her arm, and thereafter stayed very close to her side.

Victoria, still partially bemused and violently disturbed by the sadness of watching his father buried that afternoon, put her arm around him and felt an almost maternal protectiveness take possession of her as she looked down on the top of his small, sandy head. A little flame of anger leapt up in her.

"I have said that Johnny's remaining here is only a very temporary measure," she said distinctly to Georgina.

"And you yourself are about to pack your things and leave? I gather that you've just been to the funeral," flickering her luxuriant eyelashes as her glance traveled over Victoria's sober garb.

"Yes. That is to say, I've just been to the funeral, but I didn't realize I was expected to leave tonight.

As a matter of fact, Sir Peter asked me to stay on and look after Johnny.''

"What?"

"He was concerned because Johnny has just been deprived of a father, and he thought that someone he knows should stay with him for a little while. But it is only for a very little while...and in any case, I thought you knew."

"I did not. I was not consulted."

"Then I suppose it's a bit of a shock...but we shall not get in your way, I assure you. We shall take great care to keep out of your way, Miss Islesworth," and she tightened her grip on Johnny.

"But that's not the point!" The brilliant dark eyes were sparkling with emotion, and resentment and indignation flamed from them as well. "The thing that I object to is that it looks to me as if Peter, my fiancé, has been taken advantage of...that is to say, his goodness of heart has been imposed upon. Naturally, he couldn't cast the child adrift ..." with an infinitely impatient glance at the child in question. "But it's one thing to take you both in because you've been involved in an accident, and quite another to keep you both here because you're temporarily homeless. And surely the boy must have some relatives?"

"I'm afraid he hasn't," sensing Johnny's bewilderment and biting her lower lip hard.

"Not even an aunt, or an uncle—"

"No one."

"There are institutions that cope with orphans."

Even Johnny knew what the word orphan meant, and Victoria felt him clutch at her as a drowning person might clutch at a lifeline.

"Johnny may be an orphan, but he is not without friends," she stated with the same distinctness as before. "And as soon as we leave here I shall do my best to see to it that he doesn't have to be consigned to the care of an institution."

"You mean you'll look after him yourself?" with contemptuous surprise.

"If necessary."

"But you don't appear to have anywhere to take him to, or a job now that his father's dead, or very much money," with an even more contemptuous glance at the unpretentious gray suit Victoria had bought off the rack. "How will you support him, unless you work? And if you work, who will look after him?"

"I shall arrange something," Victoria replied rather helplessly.

Georgina's lip curled.

"I don't suppose the authorities will allow you to do anything of the kind," she said. "I understand they're rather hot on child welfare nowadays, and Johnny will be better off in a home. Of course he'll have to go into a home eventually."

"Please..." Victoria felt like a lioness defending her cub, "do you mind if we don't discuss this any more in front of—in front of Johnny?"

The other girl shrugged.

"As you please. But I do want you to understand quite clearly that you can't stay here.... Certainly not you yourself. The child, I suppose, will have to stay for a time, and then Sir Peter will make proper arrangements for him.'' She emphasized the word proper. "In the meantime, since Sir Peter obviously expects you to work your passage while you're here, hadn't you better put him to bed?'' She glanced at the clock on the mantelpiece. "It's six o'clock. In my nursery days all children were in bed by then, and the people employed to look after them were not allowed to skip their duties. I suggest that you go ahead with yours.''

"I will if you don't mind leaving us alone.''

Georgina looked mildly surprised. There was a certain air of dismissal about the girl in the off-the-rack suit, as well as an infinite weariness and unhappiness in her eyes. And with her soft gold hair and her pearly pallor she might have been some delicate wraith the child was clinging to.

Georgina shrugged.

"Go ahead and put him to bed. And in the morning you and I will have a talk. I think, perhaps, I might be able to find you a job.'' She paused. "What do you do when you're not looking after children?''

"I can type and do shorthand.''

"You don't look to me as if you'd make a very good secretary. Are you good at domestic duties?''

"Wh-what sort of duties?''

"My mother wants a personal maid. Do you think

you could do that sort of thing? Look after her clothes and manage her hair for her? You might even take a short course." Once again that flickering look. "You strike me as being somewhat fastidious. It's very possible you'd turn out to be a first-class personal maid."

Victoria said nothing.

Georgina started to walk toward the door, and then she turned back.

"You could visit the boy during your off-duty. I expect he'd love you to take him sweets and toys and things, when we've got him safely stowed away somewhere. You can take it from me that I shall do my utmost to persuade Sir Peter to put him in a good children's home." Once more she paused. Her look at Victoria was bright and challenging. "But whatever you do, please get it into your head that you cannot continue to take advantage of Sir Peter's kindness...and he is very, very kind to most people! As a matter of fact, he doesn't know how to say 'No' when it's a question of someone pleading poverty and tribulation."

Victoria lost what little color she had.

"I do assure you, I haven't pleaded poverty," she said with noticeable huskiness.

Georgina shrugged once more.

"Well, perhaps you simply looked at him appealingly." Her face and tone hardened. "Sir Peter Wycherley, I understand perfectly, is the sort of man to turn the head of a girl like you. He is attractive and kind and courteous and chivalrous, and in addition he's extremely wealthy—as you must have gathered from this beautiful house of his. I'm not saying you'd allow him to turn your head, but I'd rather have you out of the way...you and the child! Tomorrow I'll send for you some time during the morning and we'll discuss all the aspects of this somewhat—unusual— situation.''

Having said which, she left the room and closed the door firmly behind her, and Victoria looked down at Johnny, whose eyes were big and dark and serious.

"Doesn't that lady like us?" he asked thoughtfully.

Victoria squeezed his shoulders.

"I'm afraid she doesn't, Johnny," she admitted truthfully. "At least," she amended, in order that he shouldn't feel too shocked and perhaps alarmed, "not very much. She would prefer it if we were not here, but that's because she's going to marry Sir Peter, who has been so very kind to us both, and not unnaturally she wants us out of the way before she takes over as mistress here. I think the wedding is fairly soon, and it would show consideration for her feelings if we made our plans well before then. In fact, I think I already have an idea...." She looked at him very earnestly, hoping to encourage him by the warm smile in her eyes. "You want us to be together, don't you, Johnny?"

He answered with a mute nod of the head.

"You really mean that?" She was a trifle anxious,

in case he didn't. "After all, you don't have to come with me—"

But he nodded his head with much more vigor.

"I won't stay here without you." He clutched at her hand in such a way that she was convinced his small mind was made up on that point, at least. Wycherley Park was a haven while she was there, but it might become a dubious haven if he was deprived of her support and companionship. In any case, he had adopted her weeks ago as the next best thing to a relative. "If you go away I'm going with you—"

"Honestly? That's what you really want?"

"I like the gentleman, but I don't like the lady—"

"But you might get on very well with the lady after a time! She might be quite kind to you—let you stay here for a long time." But Victoria didn't really see that happening. "After all, this is a lovely house, and you have lots of toys and this beautiful nursery. You won't ever have such a nice place to live in again, not if you go away with me," feeling that she must make everything clear to him.

But Johnny looked suddenly indignant.

"She was horrid to you!" he spat out, as if he had bitterly resented the horridness. "You didn't do anything to make her angry, and yet she was horrid to you!" His incredulous dark eyes sought hers in complete bewilderment. "Why was she?"

Victoria shrugged.

"It doesn't matter, Johnny," she told him quietly. "I didn't in the least mind anything she said, because after all we are imposing on Sir Peter.'' At the questioning look in Johnny's eyes she explained: ''We're taking advantage of his kindness. He owes us nothing, and we are taking a lot from him—very likely making things awkward between him and Miss Islesworth. I do honestly think we should go away very soon, and since you're agreed about it we'll go together!''

Then she took him over to the wide windowseat and told him a little of what had happened that afternoon, making it quite clear to him that his father was now at rest and one day they could come back to the churchyard where he was resting and put flowers on his grave. Johnny, if he wished, could make it a place of pilgrimage in the future, and every time he did so he could put flowers on the grave.

Johnny was quite captivated by the thought of these future missions, and a great deal of the somberness—and the fear—in his dark eyes fled away after a time and left them reasonably confident and content. Johnny was too young yet to appreciate his loss, and he still had Victoria to cling to, so nothing was really bad. Not even the loss of his father, to whom he had been attached, but not passionately devoted.

But the very thought of Victoria leaving him filled him with an emotion that was an entirely different thing from the odd pang or two he had experienced as a result of the loss of his father. Victoria was Victoria!

He fell asleep after a time, and had to be wakened

for his supper, but he didn't seem to wish to eat very
much, so Victoria put him to bed. He fell asleep
again the instant his head touched the pillow, and she
had no need to read to him, or even tell him stories.
Instead she sat quietly thinking and planning and
watching the extraordinary peacefulness of his expression as he drifted into slumber.

She felt that she had been entrusted with a mission.

CHAPTER SIX

MUCH LATER THAT NIGHT she sat making calculations in her own bedroom, and decided that she had enough money, in the bank and in the post office, to keep herself and Johnny for at least two months if only she could find a place in which to live, and after that she could be successful in finding a reasonably well-paid job.

She didn't feel oppressed by the burden she had taken on when she went to bed at last, and as she lay listening to the chiming of the various grandfather and other makes of clocks that was going on around her, as well as the plushy background silence of the big house set in its stately park and grounds, she was merely mildly excited, as if she was setting out on a grand but possibly formidable adventure.

The next day she planned to take Johnny away. She would rise early, get him dressed—although unfortunately it would be impossible to feed him at that early hour—and without disturbing anyone they would steal away, much as they had come, and throw themselves upon the mercy of the world. By degrees they would return to London, and once there a bed-

sitting room would solve their immediate problems.
The welfare center where she had worked before
might help her to care for Johnny...at least while
she was working. She supposed she ought to keep in
touch with the lawyer who was handling the micro-
scopic estate—and the debts—that Johnny's father
had left to the world. There would be nothing very
much for Johnny, but at least she must keep in
touch.

That much she owed to Johmmy.

She found it impossible to sleep as the hours
crawled by. At two o'clock she got up and started
putting together her few possessions...things she
had collected while she was at Wycherley Park. And
these did not include garments that had been made
over to her by Miss Islesworth. These she returned to
the drawers and the wardrobe, where Miss Islesworth
could find them later.

At three o'clock she crept into Johnny's room and
performed the same service for him. She took the utmost care to avoid waking him, then returned to her
own room and sat watching by the window until the
first very faint light of dawn appeared in the sky.
Then she went back to Johnny's room and wakened
him.

It was difficult making the child understand that a
good deal was expected of him. He wanted to go on
slumbering contentedly in his bed, and Victoria
couldn't allow that, so she had to give him a gentle
shake occasionally.

At last she succeeded in getting him dressed, and then she had to make him understand that neither of them must make any sound. She had left a note propped up on the writing desk in her room for Sir Peter Wycherley, and in it she had thanked him for all his goodness and kindness, but made no mention of where she was going, or where she was taking Johnny. After all, or so she argued with herself, it was really no concern of his. And the relief of his fiancée when she discovered that they had gone would be incalculable.

So why did she have to let Sir Peter know where she was going?

Once they had gone—she and Johnny—he could forget them. He need never again devote a moment's thought to them, and that would completely satisfy Georgina Islesworth—Georgie as Sir Peter called her.

But Victoria always thought of her as Miss Islesworth, and under no circumstances could she ever think of her as Georgie.

Half way down the main staircase Johnny stumbled, and Victoria had to grab him quickly to prevent him from falling. The main hall was like a pool of silence, thick with shadows and glowing with the odd splashes of color created by massed flowers in copper and bronze containers. The smell of flowers and opulence lay heavily on the hushed morning atmosphere, and outside the great hall window the eastern sky flamed with cerise and banners of flamingo pink. Victoria had decided beforehand that it would be no use trying to open the great front door, for only the butler knew how to deal with the ponderous bolts and locks. Miss Islesworth was a nervous sleeper, and she liked to think that when she went to bed at night there was no danger of her repose being interrupted by housebreakers. Therefore one of the side doors— and there were quite a number of them opening on to the outside world—would have to provide them with their means of exit.

Victoria had such a strange, panic-stricken feeling that someone, or something, would prevent them getting away, and this feeling made her fingers fumble when she fought with the locks of one of the side doors—the first that they came to. This defeated her, and they went on to the next. Then, to her whole-hearted relief, they really were outside, and the exquisite, wine-like freshness of the morning, laden with the perfume of summer flowers, dew-drenched grasses and moist shrubberies, came at them, to-gether with a wild chorus of bird song that was enough to lighten anyone's heart. Victoria felt as if a load had been lifted from her shoulders, and only the future had to be coped with.

But the future was still a part of the present. Johnny moved like a sleepwalker, and the freshness of the early morning caused him to shiver noticeably. He was wearing only the T-shirt and short pants in which he'd survived the accident—Victoria prefer-ring to leave the new clothes that had been provided for him behind—and she wished that she had had the foresight to buy him a warm sweater before they left. This was an omission, however, that could be rectified as soon as they reached the world of shops.

But before they reached the world of shops there was a long drive to be traversed, and then three good miles of country road before they reached the village and the bus stop. Johnny walked with bowed shoulders and his head down, and not even the swelling chorus of birds excited him. He loved identifying bird calls, but this morning he was either acutely depressed, or very, very tired indeed, for he seemed unable to lift his eyes, and his feet dragged.

Victoria sought to encourage him. She told him that it would not be long before they reached the village inn, and then he could be provided with breakfast. And after that there would be the ride in the bus, and then a long journey by train as far as London, where he always seemed to like living. She was sure he would like to be back again among familiar scenes. . . . But Johnny merely made a supreme effort and lifted his weary eyes to her face, and she felt quite shocked as a result of what she saw in them.

"Won't we ever live in the country again?"

Victoria sought to convince him that they might one day.

"It all depends on—on a lot of things," she said. She added vaguely: "Things like whether or not I can get a job in the country. If you really want to live in the country I could try."

"But it won't be the same, will it?" Johnny persisted, peering up into her face.

"You mean there won't be a Sir Peter Wycherley to buy you things, and take you for rides in his big car?"

"I was thinking of—of the country itself," Johnny replied, waving a hand to indicate the ordered lawns on either side of them. "It won't be like this, will it? With horses and dogs, and lots and lots of flowers like there are here?"

Victoria understood perfectly.

"No, it won't," she answered truthfully. "But I did point all that out to you yesterday, didn't I?" she reminded him with just a trace of gentle rebuke in her tone.

Johnny, who had been clutching limply at her fingers, gave them a sudden squeeze.

"It's all right," he said manfully. "I don't mind."

They reached the lodgekeeper's cottage, and although it was so early a plume of smoke was rising from one of the chimneys into the pale blue of the sky, and a smell of bacon and eggs floated out to them by way of an open kitchen window.

Victoria hurried Johnny past the lodge, and then they were outside the grounds of Wycherley Park, standing on the edge of a broad, tree-shaded and extremely beautiful country road. The road, Victoria knew, was broad at this point, where the elegant gates of Wycherley Park opened out on to it, but it narrowed considerably and ran between high hedges smothered with honeysuckle and wild roses at this season of the year, and whichever way they turned they would be caught up in a wilderness of green after a few yards or so. The village of Wycherley lay to the left, so to the left they were about to turn, only the sound of a car coming from the opposite direction caused Victoria to glance round hurriedly over her shoulder, and considerably to her dismay she recognized Sir Peter Wycherley's car approaching at a reduced rate of speed.

Johnny, too, recognized the car...and he was even quicker than Victoria to recognize Sir Peter himself at the wheel. Despite the early hour he was apparently out and about, about to turn in at the gates of the Park. But the two forlorn figures standing at the side of the road deflected his purpose.

To Johnny's infinite relief—and his eyes grew several degrees brighter as he realized that a miracle had occurred (from his point of view, at any rate)—the car, with its long, sleek bonnet and effortless motion, arrived alongside of them, and Sir Peter threw open the door that was near to them and invited them to get inside.

"I don't know what you're doing up so early," he remarked, "but it's quite obvious you need a lift back to the house. Do you often do this sort of thing?" a slight smile quivering at the corners of his mouth as he addressed Victoria: "Go for long country walks at this hour of the day, I mean?"

She could have retorted by asking him whether he

often did the sort of thing he was doing on that particular morning, and left his bed before the sun was
properly up and warming the world; but she did not
do so, instead she answered with truth:

"Not often. This morning is an exception."

"I'm glad to hear it." He glanced at Johnny. "The
child looks as if he's only half awake. Wouldn't it
have been more sensible to let him enjoy the comfort
of his bed a little longer?"

Johnny told him mechanically:

"We're running away."

"You're what?"

"Running away." Johnny's eyes glistened a little
as he fixed them on the half open, inviting door of
the car. "Victoria said we had to."

"Why?"

"Because Miss Islesworth does not want us to
stay." He wriggled his fingers free of Victoria's
restraining hand and slipped on to the seat beside
the well-shaven man in the quiet suit of country
tweed. "But it's an awfully long way to the bus,
and I'm awfully hungry as well." He looked earnestly at Sir Peter. "Do you think you could take
us to the bus, sir? It would be much better than
walking!"

"Of course I'll take you to the bus." He signalled
to Victoria, and intimated that she was to take her
place in the back of the car. "After all, what is a
large car like this for, if it isn't to be placed at the
disposal of other people?"

But there was a certain wry twist to his lips as he started it up.

Victoria endeavored to explain from the back seat.

"I thought it best that we should go away. I—I—"

"Didn't even think it necessary to say goodbye?"

"Yes; of course I thought it necessary, but..." She bit her lip hard. The tweed-covered shoulders confronting her were displeased—she could tell that—and Sir Peter's shapely light brown head seemed to be set somewhat rigidly on those same shoulders, and from where she sat she could just see the angle of his very square jaw, and the slight compression at the corner of his mouth. "But I thought you might—might try to stop us...or at any rate, that you might try and prevent me taking Johnny away."

"And you're quite certain Johnny is unhappy at Wycherley Park?"

"Oh no, no! But Miss Islesworth—"

"Miss Islesworth doesn't in the least object to my keeping Johnny at the Park."

"No, but I know she does object to my staying there, too, and looking after him. And you know very well that it's only a very temporary thing... Johnny staying with you. In a few weeks he'll have to go away."

"When?"

His tone was so dry and interested that she found it difficult to answer.

"When—when you're married, Sir Peter."

"Oh, is that all?" They were cruising along at a very moderate rate of speed for such a powerful car, and he turned and looked at her over his shoulder. "If you were Miss Islesworth would you object to Johnny staying on after you were married?"

"No, but I'm—I'm not Miss Islesworth."

"True." The narrow lane was a series of unexpected twists and bends, and he negotiated them carefully, frowning as he did so. "You are not Miss Islesworth.... You are Miss Victoria Wood! And I can't think why you had to get up so early in order to disappear out of my life! Wouldn't a more reasonable hour have satisfied you just as well?"

"I—I—You might have tried to prevent me!"

"That's true," he agreed again.

"And it seemed the best thing to do...."

"Even though Johnny is very small, and it's quite a long way to the village...and the bus I presume you intend to take?"

"Yes, but—"

"However, we'll have you at the bus much more quickly in this car, won't we?" This time he glanced at Johnny, and Johnny was so happy sitting beside him in such a splendid means of transport that he grinned expansively.

"Yes," he said, plainly without any thought of the bus.

"But first we'll have breakfast at the George and Dragon." They drew up beside the white-fronted hostelry, and as the sun was climbing high in the sky by this time it all looked very serene and mellow with the golden rays bathing it in a kind of golden balm, and the giant oak tree in the center of the village providing a delicious form of shade for a contingent of ducks that were parading as a matter of routine, and in order to discover their own breakfast. "I know the man who runs this place, and he always gets up early, so he won't mind cooking us bacon and eggs. And I expect you'd like a rather generous sized plateful, wouldn't you, Johnny, after walking all the way down my two-mile drive?"

Johnny agreed, showing a gap in his teeth as he smiled again as if he had discovered Elysium.

"And toast and marmalade," he added, in case it should be forgotten. "And tea. I like tea," he confided.

Sir Peter agreed with him that there was nothing like a pot of tea in the early morning.

"We English don't go in much for coffee," he observed conversationally. "Or not seriously. Certainly not in the early morning."

"Victoria said we'd have breakfast at the inn, but I didn't think we'd get there very quickly," the child admitted, dropping his eyes to his own small feet, as if he recognized their deficiencies.

Sir Peter laid a lead brown hand on his knee.

"Poor Johnny!" he said.

Then he glanced quickly over his shoulder.

"Poor Miss Wood!" he added, before helping them both to alight.

CHAPTER SEVEN

VICTORIA HAD ALWAYS THOUGHT that an English inn in the heart of really beautiful and peaceful country, with wonderful views opening out on either hand, and the scent of flowers and wood smoke and perhaps even cow manure coming in at the open front door—particularly in the early morning—was a really wonderful place.

She didn't frequent them, and she had only once stayed in such a place, but she considered that its picture postcardlike qualities far outweighed any inconveniences, such as the lack of running hot water in the bedrooms, and central heating in the winter time. They were traditional places, redolent of history, and when they had an enormous oak tree not far from their front porch it all added to the picturesqueness.

Johnny was intrigued by the George and Dragon because it had a connection with one of his favorite heroes, and the waiter who brought their breakfast told him that it had once been a favorite hideout for highwaymen, and anything more exciting and satisfying than that Johnny couldn't think of.

He ate his breakfast with an appetite that proved

he had recovered entirely from the depression that had held him from the moment he opened his eyes that morning, and while his two companions ploughed more sedately through similar fare he chattered in such a way that the silences which might have existed between the other two—at any rate, during the opening stages of the meal—were not possible under the constant fire of his questions, and his eager comments on his surroundings and the amount of toast he could consume once his early morning lassitude had departed.

Victoria wished he wouldn't talk quite so much since she herself felt strangely bewildered...not entirely surprising since she had scarcely closed her eyes all night. But Peter Wycherley was obviously both amused and intrigued by the childish chatter. He encouraged Johnny to talk as much and as continuously as he pleased, and only when they arrived at the stage of the meal when he lit a cigarette, and Victoria declined to follow suit, did he revert to the subject of their imminent departure and the possible arrival of the bus.

"You really are determined to take the boy back to London?" he inquired politely of Victoria. But as he sat studying her through the faint haze of smoke his cigarette had created, she was quite unconvinced by his expression that he either approved or disapproved of her decision.

"Yes," she answered, toying with a fragment of toast.

"You don't think the amenities at Wycherley Park are quite up to standard?"

"Don't be silly." She flushed brilliantly. "Of course Wycherley Park is wonderful, and Johnny has thoroughly enjoyed staying with you. But we both know that staying at Wycherley Park is rather like living in a dreamworld, a purely temporary dreamworld. And the sooner we both return to normal the better."

"For you as well as Johnny?"

"Y-yes." Her long eyelashes hid her eyes as she stared downwards at the toast, and her nervous fingers continued to maltreat it. "For me even more than Johnny. Johnny is a child and will soon forget. He'll adapt wherever we go. But I.... You see," raising her eyes hastily to his strangely serene gray ones, "I used to live in the country, and I've always wanted to—to get back to it. I don't really like towns."

"But you think Johnny does?"

"N-no...."

"I hate towns." Johnny spoke with emphasis. "Even the parks are not real country, and there are always park keepers who won't let you play on the grass."

"And you think my head gardener doesn't object when you damage my flower beds with your cricket balls?" His almost languid glance swept to the child.

"I like your head gardener. He's jolly nice." Johnny, who had made many friends among the staff at Wycherley Park during his stay there, was emphatic on this point. "I like your cook, and Florrie, the housemaid. They're jolly nice, too."

"I'm relieved to hear it." The man's shapely mouth smiled. "Personally, I get along very well with both of them. But one likes to have outside opinions."

Johnny rattled on about the cook making him gingerbread men with currants for eyes, and he seemed to have a lot of information on the subject of Florrie's latest boyfriend—and apparently she went in for quantity rather than quality—which he was quite eager to impart, but Victoria interrupted with reminders that the bus was due at any moment, and Johnny looked dashed.

"Do we have to catch it?" he protested. "Why can't we wait for another?"

"Yes, why not?" Sir Peter extracted another cigarette from his case and lighted it leisurely. "After all, what's the hurry?"

"We have to catch a train." Victoria, who had looked up details of train services in the timetable, felt as if her nerves were tightly stretched pieces of wire, and Sir Peter was trying them too far. If they missed that train they would have to wait hours for another.

"There must by any number of trains making their way to London from the provinces day after day." Sir Peter was lying back comfortably in his chair, and he had even ordered another pot of tea. "I simply

cannot understand why you have to catch one particular train.''

"I've already told you, we—we're leaving.'' She
fought hard to control the tremble in her voice, and
the color on her cheekbones was agitated. "Don't
you see, Sir Peter.... It's like having a tooth extracted. The sooner you go to the dentist's the better
when you know it's got to come out!''

"But you're only returning to London because you
think Miss Islesworth doesn't want you at Wycherley
Park.''

"She doesn't.''

"How can you be certain?''

"She—she said so.''

"Did she?'' Sir Peter looked interested. They
heard the rumble of the bus, and Johnny ran out to
make absolutely certain it really was the bus and not
a heavy truck that was unloading stores at the inn. As
soon as he was out of earshot the owner of Wycherley Park spoke incisively. "Give the child another
day, Miss Wood...just one more day! I promise I'll
take you to the station myself if you elect to leave
tomorrow, but for this one day—and it's going to be
a remarkably fine one!'' glancing at the windows—
"forget that you have any pressing problems, and
make up your mind to relax in sylvan solitude. I'm
going to take you both for a drive, and I promise to
show you something interesting. I think Johnny will
find it very interesting! You, too, if you'll stop thinking about dreary places like railway stations, and

London parks where the park keepers won't let live wires like Johnny play on the strips of dried-up grass.''

"The grass in London parks is not dried up.'' Victoria felt she had to defend it,...after all, she had been thankful for London parks many times in her career. "And park keepers have a lot to try them. Even Johnny can be trying sometimes.''

"But not so trying that you wish to be separated from him?''

"Of course not!''

"Then I think you ought to grant me this one day at least.''

"But won't Miss—? What about Miss Islesworth?''

"Her mother is arriving by the afternoon train, and they'll have a lot to talk about. This morning she has an appointment with the hairdresser.''

"So you are free to devote yourself to other causes?'' Victoria could have bitten out her tongue as soon as she had spoken, and she simply couldn't understand why she was being so unfair. He had been more than good to herself and Johnny, and she had absolutely no right to feel either irritation or a most peculiar sensation that was almost like envy as she leveled what was almost an accusation. And certainly her tone was a trifle acid.''

"If you put it like that, yes.''

They had both risen and walked to the window to look through it for Johnny, and she knew that the sudden coolness in his eyes was well merited as he turned to survey her. So was the faint hint of reproach.

"I—I'm sorry." In an apologetic rush the words poured out. "I don't really know how to thank you for all you've done for Johnny during his stay in your house, and I realize I must sound extraordinarily ungrateful just because—"

"Yes?" he prompted. "Just because. . .?" And he went on watching her.

"Oh, I suppose because it can't continue." She flushed more brilliantly than ever as she decided to be truthful. "You've done so much. But it has to end. I'm devoted to Johnny, and I want him to have all the advantages and the opportunities that he can get from life, but I realize he mustn't expect to receive them at your hands. Your obligation—and it was never really an obligation—is finished, done with! When you take us to the station tomorrow you'll probably never see either of us again."

"You make it sound very final," he said.

"Well, it is final." She straightened her slim back against the wall. Her blue eyes were almost defiant. "Sir Peter, I think we ought to go today."

The bus was on the point of leaving outside the inn, and Johnny was standing in the road and having a conversation with the bus driver.

"That child likes making contacts," Sir Peter observed, and smiled briefly as he glanced toward him. Then he turned back to the girl with the light gold hair who was making a supreme effort not to betray the fact that she felt very much like crying because she had hardly slept all night, she was responsible for Johnny, and the future loomed ahead of her, crammed with all sorts of difficulties. Even the small sum she had in the bank was smaller than she had believed when she checked up on it the preceding day. "By the way, if you don't mind my inquiring, how do you propose to support Johnny when you get to London?" the landowner asked. "And if on top of that the question doesn't strike you as impertinent, where do you propose to live?"

"We—we'll live somewhere."

"But **at** the moment you're not quite sure where."

"No."

"I assume that you have to have a job?"

"Yes."

"At at the moment you haven't got one?"

"No."

"Yet you still think Wycherley Park is not the right place for a temporary refuge?"

"Yes." She was so sure of it that the amount of emphasis she laid on the word startled her.

"Very well." Sir Peter turned, and as Johnny came running in at the open door he took him by the hand and led him out again into the sunshine. Victoria was not really surprised that the innkeeper did not present a bill for their breakfast, and Sir Peter merely turned to him and waved a hand and said casually, "See you later, Bill."

"Aye, aye, sir," Bill—who had been in the Mer-

chant Navy before he took to innkeeping—answered
cheerfully.

The long, gleaming car was still outside the inn,
and Sir Peter opened both doors so that they could
climb in. Johnny took it for granted that he was once
more to occupy the passenger seat beside the driving
seat, and Victoria made herself comfortable on the
rear seat. She did not actually make herself comfortable, for her backbone felt too stiff to enable her to
relax, but she lay back very slightly and clasped her
hands in her lap, and waited for the moment when
the wind would sing past her ears and all the freshness of the day would once more encompass her.

The car was an open one, and Sir Peter seemed to
think she might need a rug over her knees. He handed
her one, and she automatically laid it lightly over her
knees. They started off, and the proprietor of the
George and Dragon watched them with some interest
from the top of the short flight of steps that led up to
the inn door, and Johnny glanced back over his
shoulder and waved to the man addressed as 'Bill,'
and Victoria marveled that he seemed entirely happy.
He had been promised a day out, and he was prepared to enjoy it. . .the bogey of the railway train
and London had receded.

But Victoria knew this was only a very temporary
reprieve.

They returned along the road by which they had
come, but when they reached the gates of Wycherley
Park Sir Peter ignored them, and they swept on along

the narrowing lane and deep into the heart of enchanting country.

The day was full of gentle breezes and really strong, warm sunshine, and very soon Victoria found it necessary to discard her coat as well as the rug, and Johnny was delighted because he was not burdened with a coat. Even Sir Peter, after a time, removed his coat and rolled up his shirt sleeves, and they went on like a small contingent of happy holidaymakers until the position of the sun in the sky informed Victoria that it was nearly noon. Then Sir Peter swung the car off the main road and they delved deep into a labyrinth of leafy lanes and thickets of tangled green until the silken gleam of a river showed up, and on a stretch of cool, sweet grass beside the river Sir Peter stopped the car and the passengers were invited to alight.

Johnny needed no invitation, for he was actually out of the car and running beside the river before Victoria fully realized that this was to be a halt. Then, as she alighted slowly and somewhat stiffly, she looked up at the man for an explanation.

"It's very beautiful here," she commented, "but we've come a long way to admire a strip of river."

"And now that you're here you don't admire it?" He glanced at her somewhat sharply.

"But of course!" She gazed upward into the dim green of the leaves above her head, and the softest of breezes made her skin feel cool and revived, somehow. She could hear the slumbrous gurgle of the

river, and occasionally something went 'plop'—a fish
most likely—and the silken surface of the water was
marred by a series of ripples. She gazed at it as if it
hypnotized her, and she watched a kingfisher darting
among the reeds and was reminded of a brilliant
brooch flashing through the air. "Of course!" she
repeated, with enthusiaism, and in the iris-blue
depths of her eyes a glow of appreciation showed up
very plainly. "But I didn't know you had so much
time on your hands that you could afford to waste
some of it by bringing Johnny and me here."

"When you might have been on your way to London?" He smiled at her with an attractive little quirk
at one corner of his mouth, and he went round to the
back of the car and lifted out a hamper. "I asked
Bill, at the George and Dragon, to put us up some
lunch," he explained. "He's pretty good at carrying
out orders—mine, at any rate—and I suspect that
he's taken into consideration the fact that Johnny
has a pretty large appetite."

He called to Johnny.

"Here, come and open this, and find out what
we've got!"

Johnny abandoned his pursuit of the kingfisher
and came racing back. Eagerly he pounced on the
hamper while Victoria, for a reason she herself didn't
understand, continued to make it plain that she was
puzzled by the proceedings, and she was sure that
Miss Islesworth, if she was aware of them, would not
be at all pleased.

Sir Peter's brow creased as she asked him in a very direct manner whether he thought his fiancée would approve. He shrugged his shirt-clad shoulders.

"Probably not, but I don't seek Miss Islesworth's approval of everything I do." For a short while she thought there was actual impatience in his eyes as they dwelt on her, and she was surprised that the normally serene gray depths could display quite so much obvious irritation. And it was irritation because she was refusing to fall in with his mood...which seemed a strange one to her, needing a certain amount of explanation. "After all, I don't interfere with her when she goes off to the hairdresser's, or does things she wants to do on her own. Marriage— when you've got as far as the stage of seriously contemplating it—is a partnership, not a sacrifice of freedom in exchange for a term of bondage."

"Yes, I see," Victoria observed, regarding him thoughtfully. "That's the way you look at it, is it?"

"That's the way I look at it," with another of his brief, one-sided smiles. For the first time faintly contemptuous, or so she thought.

The hamper contained a cold chicken and a flask of coffee, rolls, fruits and biscuits, and Johnny for one was not slow in demolishing his share of it. Despite the enormous breakfast he had consumed he seemed to have little difficulty in accounting for the better part of a wing of chicken following a generous slice of melon, and as Bill had thoughtfully included some bottles of pop for him he was very soon lying

on his small back on the turf and vowing that he
wouldn't be able to move for hours and hours.

Sir Peter glanced at his watch from time to time,
and seemed to be dwelling upon their next move even
while he stared at the river. The sheer brightness of it
had a soporific effect on Victoria, and although she
ate far less than Johnny she would have welcomed a
long, lazy period devoted to doing nothing at all—
not even consciously thinking very much while the
brilliance of the river exerted its influence—after the
crumbs were gathered up and the cap screwed on the
coffee flask. But Sir Peter, who had been the one to
lead them to this halycon spot, and had not hesitated
to proclaim it ideal for whiling away the better por-
tion of a hot summer day, seemed to become galva-
nized into action when he realized they were both
about to close their eyes and drift into slumber.

"We must go," he said, leaping to his feet. "Delightful though this is, we haven't the time to waste
sitting here. We have something else to do."

"What?" Victoria inquired, looking up at him
through half-closed eyes.

He looked down at her with a quizzical expression
on his face.

"Do you always have to be told everything in advance?" he asked.

A spirit of perverseness and a desire to be pro-
vocative entered into her.

"You didn't tell me where we were going before
you brought us here," she reminded him.

"No. But then I wasn't entirely certain I was going to bring you here."

"Why did you bring us here?"

"Because it's a favorite spot of mine. Because I used to come here a lot when I was—well, not much older than Johnny's age." He looked up and down the river with a reminiscent expression in his face. "I used to enjoy myself in those days." He lit a cigarette thoughtfully. "I've also known unhappiness on this spot, and uncertainty."

"Uncertainty?"

"Yes." He met the limpid blueness of her eyes. "Paralyzing uncertainty."

"But apparently you recovered from it? You discovered the way out?"

"I'm not at all certain it was the right way out. However—" he cast away the cigarette—"I choose now to believe that it was. Or I'm trying very hard to believe that it was. Shall we go?"

"If you think we ought to."

She allowed him to help her to her feet, and as he surveyed her thoughtfully she dusted down the front of her dress with her hands.

"Where are we going? Home?"

"But you haven't a home," he reminded her. "Only this morning you planned to start looking for one. Remember?"

She nodded mutely. Despite his apparent kindness he could be a little cruel sometimes...for surely it was cruel to remind her that she was temporarily without a home? Not even the most humble kind of roof over her head!

It very soon appeared to her that they were returning by the way they had come. There were the same leafy lanes closing round them, the same offshoots from those lanes, deep and silent woods. The car proceeded so cautiously after a time that Victoria began to fear they were lost—and she had more than once feared this on the outward journey.

But very soon it became apparent that they were not lost. Sir Peter had been searching for something, and after about an hour's driving he found it—or rather, its extremely ancient roof peered at him about the top of an extremely high hedge.

Victoria looked up at the mellow red tiles and the twisted chimney pots, and she was just about to exclaim that it looked like an abode of witches—or fairies—when the car stopped. It stopped right outside a small, white-painted garden gate, and at the end of a long garden path the cottage stood waiting.

"We get out here," Sir Peter said.

CHAPTER EIGHT

JOHNNY WAS ENCHANTED. The heat of the afternoon and the after-effects of the generous lunch he had consumed had induced a strong feeling of drowsiness in his case, and he had been dozing intermittently for the past forty minutes, but the sight of the cottage aroused him from his slumberous condition with a kind of jerk.

He sat bolt upright in his seat beside the driver and rubbed his eyes to make certain he wasn't seeing things.

"It looks like Hansel and Gretel's cottage," he observed.

"Only it happens to be mine." Sir Peter smiled at him. "Like to see over it?"

Johnny was charmed by the notion. All at once he was fully and broadly awake.

Victoria slid out of the car before Sir Peter could open the rear door for her. She was leaning on the cottage gate when he came up behind her.

"Is it really yours?" She looked up at him curiously. "The garden seems very neglected, but the cottage is adorable. I love that uneven roof. Is it very old?"

"Very old. It was almost certainly standing here when an ancestor of mine who returned from Agincourt was laying the foundations of the original Wycherley Park."

"Then the present Wycherley Park is not the original?"

"No. Parts of it have been preserved in the present structure, but only parts."

"This cottage—" she waved a hand to indicate it—"appears to be unoccupied, although there are curtains at the windows."

"That's right. I leased it to a man and his wife who own a rubber plantation in Malaya for their home leave, but that was six months ago, and it has remained untenanted since. Like to look over it?"

"Why?" She was unable to tell quite why, but she felt extremely suspicious. Although the cottage was enchanting, and she would love to see over it, she simply couldn't understand why he should waste time on the homeward journey to even suggest they might like to look over his cottage. From her point of view time was valuable, and if she and Johnny had to catch a train after all...after so much wasted time....

But Johnny was impatient. He hopped about on one foot and demanded that they see over the cottage as quickly as possible if Sir Peter had the key. Sir Peter produced the key from his pocket.

"You can turn it in the lock yourself, Johnny, if you like," he said, as he opened the gate and led the way up the garden path. "I promise you there's nothing inside to alarm you, not even a few bats, for I had it cleaned and tidied up only a week or so ago."

For what purpose? Victoria wondered.

She received enlightenment very soon.

They prowled all over the cottage, which was genuine Tudor and as delightful a small and cosy cottage as Victoria knew she was ever likely to have the privilege of inspecting. The furnishings were very simple, but entirely adequate, and what pleased her feminine eye almost more than anything else was the condition of the doll's-houselike kitchen, which appeared to be equipped with everything that was essential in the way of modern amenities.

The people from Malaya must have had a very pleasant time during their occupation of the cottage and they had dealt with it lovingly while they were there. There were only two bedrooms—one very small indeed, and the other not very much larger—and in the larger of the two they had left a relic of their more permanent home, a gaily-dressed Malaysian doll. It was sitting on the dressing table, and Johnny pounced on it.

Sir Peter told him he could have it if he wanted it, and while he and Victoria inspected an entirely adequate airing-cupboard, an apple storage area and a bathroom, Johnny wandered out into the garden with his new possession. Sir Peter led the way back to the sitting room, that was bright with chintz and one or two nicely polished articles of furniture, and asked Victoria what she thought of the place.

She answered him truthfully:

"I love it. But it doesn't really matter what I think of it, does it?"

He looked down at her a little quizzically. She was conscious of sounding ungracious, and she looked defensive.

"It does matter, because I'm about to offer it to you as a place in which to reside...oh, only temporarily, of course." He saw her mouth fall open, and he understood her astonishment. "Naturally, since it's somewhat isolated, I'm not asking you to live here permanently, but your situation at the moment is that you require somewhere to live. You don't appear to relish the idea of continuing to live at Wycherley Park, and I need someone to take charge of Johnny. I don't mind telling you," regarding her with rather more of a frown, "that I don't at all approve of your intention to take Johnny to London. For one thing he is no connection of yours, and for another I intend to adopt him. So you see, you were behaving reprehensibly when you attempted to carry him off!"

"You intend to...adopt him?" She could hardly believe the evidence of her ears.

He nodded.

"You seem surprised. But someone has to look after him, and with all the will in the world I don't think you have the means to do so. I have the means, the will...and the blessing of the welfare center in London where Johnny was once cared for. Naturally, it will take time before adoption papers can be made out, and Johnny is my official responsibility; but already the wheels have been set in motion to achieve that end, and my immediate problem is to find someone who will devote themselves to Johnny and insure his physical well-being until such time as I can make arrangements for him to be sent away to school. I understand that he will be nine next birthday, and it's high time he was sent to a good character-molding school.''

"Eton, perhaps?" She said it very dryly because she knew he couldn't possibly mean any such establishment.

"There are other schools beside Eton, although it's true I went there myself. And it would be necessary for his name to have been put down at birth, so we'll have to rule that one out.''

Victoria groped for a chair and sat down on it rather suddenly.

"You really mean you would—if you could—send him to Eton?" she demanded.

He shrugged.

"If I could. But I can't, so there's not much point in discussing what I can't do, is there?''

"And Miss Islesworth?" Just as all roads at one time led to Rome so any discussion with Sir Peter about Johnny inevitably led to Georgina Islesworth. "Does she know about this?" Victoria inquired a trifle huskily.

Sir Peter looked vaguely irritated.

"Miss Islesworth and I plan to be married some time next year," he explained, "and since you insist upon knowing, I have gone into the problems of Johnny with her. She knows I intend—and I repeat intend!—to adopt him, and make myself responsible for the whole of his future. I'm afraid I'm unable to tell you that she entirely approves, but that is my resolution, and she respects it." As Victoria stared at him: "It may seem strange to you, but there is a good deal of give and take about marriage, and Miss Islesworth has yielded ground on this particular issue. I have her word that she will not interfere."

Victoria simply couldn't believe it.

"And when your own children arrive...?" She posed the question a little haltingly, and with diffidence. "What difference will that make?"

"None at all to Johnny."

"You mean he'll be accepted? Looked upon as a member of your own family?"

"Of course," a certain amount of cold hauteur in his tone. "I thought I had made myself absolutely clear on that point already."

Victoria sat gripping the arms of her chair—rather a hard wooden one that was nevertheless a period piece. Outside in the garden, among the tangle of weeds and old-fashioned roses, lilies and virginia stock run riot, Johnny chased a butterfly and disappeared round an angle of the house. They could hear his shrill voice calling excitedly, and it was already abundantly clear that he had taken to the cottage as a duck takes to water. Wycherley Park or a small Tudor cottage enclosed by silent woods and lush pastures...to Johnny they were apparently one and the same, since both belonged to Sir Peter Wycherley. And in his small mind it was apparently perfectly natural that the cottage should belong to Sir Peter, and as a result he already felt at home.

Johnny had achieved security.

And, unknown to Johnny, he had achieved a very great deal of security.

But Victoria could still not believe it.

"It's bound to lead to trouble," she predicted. "A child like Johnny, and someone like Miss Islesworth!"

"You mean that you would prefer it if I allowed you to keep Johnny? If permission was granted to you to toil and slave for him?" But despite the picture he painted of her working hard in Johnny's interests there was only a kind of cool, contemptuous disapproval in his voice. "Why, my dear Miss Wood," Sir Peter pointed out, 'you are not even married!"

"And what difference does that make?" defensively.

He shrugged again.

"No difference, since you are not nearly old enough to be Johnny's mother. However, some people might decide you merely look young."

She flushed.

"I could always say that he was my brother."

"But when my adoption papers are made absolute he will be my adopted son!"

"And you really—really mean to adopt him?"

"I have said so," in frozen tones.

"And you want me to stay on here and look after him, until he goes away to school?"

"I think it would be a good idea," he agreed, "particularly as you have nowhere to live. This cottage can be made over to you for the time being, and as it's very small it should be quite easy to run. If you want any help with cooking, and that sort of thing, I'm sure there's some woman in the village who can provide it. And naturally you will receive a salary for looking after Johnny, and all your expenses will be met by myself. I have had the contents of the cottage checked, and there's everything here for your needs. . . plenty of linen, etc. I don't expect you to become a drudge, but I think you should enjoy running the place as if it was your own home—which, in fact, it can be until you elect to move on!—and taking care of Johnny. As it's the summer holidays he won't need to attend school for the time being, and he can have a grand time here running wild in the garden. You can take life easily yourself, look upon it as a kind of holiday job—"

"Thank you," she returned, a trifle stiffly—in fact, very stiffly. "I shall certainly look upon it as a job."

He regarded her somewhat strangely.

"It occurred to me that you might enjoy being here...you as well as Johnny!"

She realized that he was providing both Johnny and herself with a kind of hideout—somewhere where they would be out of sight, though possibly not entirely out of mind of his fiancée. And the knowledge that, despite his protestations, they had to be kept hidden instead of enjoying the amenities of Wycherley Park quite openly incensed her unreasonably.

Later she was to feel less resentful, and more appreciative; but while he stood there leaning against the mantelpiece—a beamed affair decorated with shining horse brasses—and peering at her in that vaguely perplexed, vaguely concerned, vaguely irritated manner which overlooked the fact that she had the right to make her own decisions and lead her own life—and take care of Johnny, if she chose, until some official decision was made about him, a sense of rebellion stirred in her. She wished Johnny was not quite so enthusiastic when he came rushing in from the garden with the excited piece of information that he had found a pony in the paddock.

Sir Peter smiled at him.

"I thought you might like to learn to ride, Johnny," he said. "And you can take charge of the pony and groom it. There are stable quarters round at the back of the cottage, with feeding stuffs and so on. It will be your job to be responsible for the pony...whose name, by the way, is Thomas."

Johnny was even more wildly excited.

"Why Thomas?"

"Why not?" Sir Peter tweaked his ear. "Anyway, he's yours, and there are lots of other things in this cottage that you can look upon as yours. Books and things...I had brought over from the Park."

It occured to Victoria to walk out into the kitchen and examine the kitchen cupboards. She found that they were well stocked with foodstuffs, and, in fact, there was everything they could possibly need in the cottage. Sir Peter had been quite thorough in his preparations for their occupancy.

The only things that were missing were the personal things—the clothes, toys, etc—that had been bought for Johnny and which had been left behind at Wycherley Park. But even these were to be brought over from the big house, and Sir Peter's own chauffeur had received instructions to call at the cottage once or twice a week to make absolutely certain they had everything they needed.

"And if you feel you want to go for a drive Hawkins will take you wherever you wish to go while he is here," Sir Peter told them, before he turned toward the door.

Victoria suddenly realized that he intended to leave them there, and that his intention was that they should settle into the cottage without leaving it again—and without time for reflection on her part.

He had taken it for granted that she would fall in with his wishes, and because of Johnny she realized

that she had no alternative but to fall in with them.
She didn't quite understand herself at that phase of
her existence, for the cottage was something she had
often dreamed about in the past, and apparently
nothing was to be lacking that could make for her
and Johnny's comfort. Sir Peter had informed them
that they were less than a mile from the village, and
as there was a telephone laid in the cottage they were
not really in the least cut off...and in emergency
there was always Sir Peter Wycherley himself, at
Wycherley Park.

In the event of anything going wrong, or if she was
worried about anything, she was to contact him at
once.

Johnny could hardly believe that they were actually to take up residence in the cottage, and that for
several weeks at least it was to be his home.

Far, far nicer this than a dreary London bedsitting
room. He raced delightedly out to the car when Sir
Peter intimated that he was leaving. Hawkins was to
bring the rest of their things over that evening, and
they were already as good as installed.

Sir Peter chucked Johnny under the chin before he
slipped behind the wheel of his car, and he once more
pinched his ear.

"Look after Miss Wood, Johnny," he ordered
him, "and I have no doubts at all that Miss Wood
will look after you very well indeed!"

Then he slid in his clutch, smiled fleetingly and
rather peculiarly at Victoria—and, not for the first

time, she thought what unusually attractive and
rather charming gray eyes he had—waved a careless
hand that included them both in a dismissing wave,
and drove off.

They were alone in a leafy paradise that was heavy
with the scent of roses and murmurous with the droning of bees. And, apart from that insistent droning of
bees, the silence—once Sir Peter's car had disappeared down the lane—was a silence that could be
felt.

CHAPTER NINE

THEY WITHDREW INSIDE the cottage after standing together at the gate for a few minutes, and Victoria began a more detailed inspection of the cottage.

While Sir Peter was there, and under the somewhat quizzical—when he wasn't looking strangely impatient—gaze of his gray eyes, she had felt disinclined to betray any real interest, but now that they were alone it was a different matter. All women are curious about houses, and the contents of houses, and Victoria was no exception. Never in the whole of her life (leaving out the short period of it that had been passed at Wycherley Park) had she seen anything as compact and as beautifully equipped as the cottage. The furnishings were simple, but the materials used for curtains and chair covers and bed covers were expensive and tasteful. One found them in places like Liberty's and Harrod's furnishing departments.

The best bedroom was full of eggshell blue highly glazed chintz. The tiny room next door—Johnny's room—was also blue, but a rather more decided color, likely to appeal to a boy of eight years old. The sitting room—which was also the dining room of the cottage—was a symphony of faded pinks, lavender and leaf green. There was an elegant little bureau in one corner, a gate-legged table in the center of the carpet, a highly polished sideboard stood against the farther wall, and a grandfather clock ticked at the foot of the stairs.

On the upstairs landing there was another grandfather clock. The whole minute space echoed to the solemn ticking of the two clocks.

There was no television or radio, but there was a very large number of books. And as Sir Peter had promised to send them over a small transistor radio this solved all Johnny's problems.

Victoria was intrigued by the kitchen equipment, and felt an urge to try out the stove. She was, on the whole, a very good cook, and as Johnny soon declared himself in need of supper she got down to the task of preparing something for him.

In the kitchen cupboards there was a large number of tins. The refrigerator contained eggs, butter and milk, and the preparation of an omelette seemed the obvious solution to supper. Johnny had eaten so well all day that he was not really hungry, and halfway through his supper his eyelids dropped and he was plainly more ready for bed than anything else.

Victoria had been assured that the beds were well aired, and she put Johnny to bed before washing up the supper things. Then, while the child slumbered peacefully with his sandy head on yet another strange pillow, and the grandfather clocks went on ticking

away against a background whirr that indicated they
were prepared to chime the quarters as well as the
half hours and hours, she tidied up the living room
and, as it was a really beautiful night, went out into
the garden.

All around her were apple trees, pear trees, and
thickets of soft fruit. As well as weeds that grew waist
high there were a large number of flowers, and the
warm night air was staturated with the penetrating
scent of clove-pinks and honeysuckle. The honeysuckle clambered riotously over the high garden wall,
and from the spinney on the other side of the road
opposite the garden gate came the exciting song of a
nightingale.

Victoria listened, realizing that it was the first time
she had heard a nightingale for a long time. Even at
Wycherley Park, where the gardens were so well
tended that there were few thickets to provide hide-
outs for song birds, she had listened in vain for just
such a sound during more than one of her nightly
walks in the grounds. But here, where the silence was
intense and no one had bothered about the garden
for weeks, the melodious and unmistakable soft trill
of the sweetest of all musically minded feathered
creatures poured out in an eager rush, and continued
almost without cessation while Victoria stood leaning
on the garden gate and listening to it.

The silence of the white road that curved beyond
the gate fascinated her. She supposed that if she had
been town-bred like Johnny she would have been a

little frightened by it...or at any rate, faintly perturbed. She might even have mistrusted it, and
despite the glimmering golden moon that was climbing into the sky above the rambling orchard and the
fields that lay behind it, have panicked and rushed
back into the house and bolted and barred the door
against any possible menaces that the night might
hold for herself and Johnny, who was upstairs and
fast asleep.

But being country-bred she had no fears whatsoever, and she leaned on the gate quite happily, and
thought how deliciously soft the night air was, and
how vaguely exciting the dusk that crowded close to
her beneath the trees. A bat describing circles in the
clear blue above the bending boughs of a buddleia
made a sudden swoop and all but skimmed her
cheek, but it didn't upset her at all. She was not
afraid of bats, not afraid that one might get caught
up in her hair...anymore than she was afraid of the
loneliness and the dark.

She looked up through the boughs of the buddleia
and saw the golden globe of the moon swimming in a
sea of soft blue light, and she thought of Byron's
"She walks in beauty like the night," and Tenny-
son's "How bright the moon on Cumnor Hall," and
thought that if she was a poet she would compose
endless verses about the moon and the effects of
moonlight on human beings—particularly at the full
of the moon—and other creatures that were not
generally supposed to have the same reactions as

human beings. And, more than anything else, she would dwell upon the sheer, sensuous delight of moonlight.

But, not being a poet, she decided to go indoors and early to bed, and in the morning she would have to draw up some sort of plan for her own and Johnny's daily life as long as they were at the cottage.

Just before she went indoors and wisely secured all the bolts—not because of sudden nervousness but because of common sense—she thought she really did hear a rather curious noise which reached her from the main road, and after a few seconds she could quite easily have deceived herself into believing that she was listening to footsteps ringing rather hollowly on the smooth surface of the road.

Then, with a light shrug of her shoulders, she dismissed the sound, and drove home the bolts.

After all, what if it was some country wayfarer making his way home after an evening at the inn in the village? Or after spending an evening with friends! It was really nothing to do with her! Nothing at all.

She looked in on Johnny before entering her own room, and was pleased because he was sleeping so profoundly that he made absolutely no movement, and his arms were flung wide, embracing the whole of his enchanting small room, as it were.

The next day was a more strenuous day than Victoria had known for a long time. She got up early and cooked Johnny a really substantial breakfast, while contenting herself with fruit juice and cereal, and after breakfast started making a list of all the things that they had to purchase at the vllage shop. Sir Peter had given her clearly to understand that it was about a mile from the cottage, and they set off to walk the distance with two pairs of equally enthusiastic and curious feet.

Actually, it was much more like two miles, but neither Victoria nor Johnny minded in the least, and even the thought of the return journey didn't deter them.

But before commencing the return journey they made the acquaintance of the butcher and the grocer in the village, as well as the postmistress, who seemed a little curious when she learned where it was that they were staying.

"Alder Cottage? But I thought it was still empty." She peered curiously at Victoria. "You must have moved in rather suddenly!"

"We moved in yesterday," Victoria informed her while she slipped a book of stamps inside her handbag.

The postmistress's eyebrows rose.

"I didn't know Sir Peter was going to let it. I didn't know he'd made up his mind what to do with it."

"He hasn't let it," Victoria further informed her. "Johnny—" she prevented him upsetting a bowl of eggs on the counter— "is Sir Peter's ward, and I'm looking after him." She couldn't think of any reason why she had to keep Johnny's new security secret from the rest of the world. "We shall probably be at the cottage for a few weeks."

"Indeed!" But the way the postmistress said it this was tremendous news. "I didn't know Sir Peter had a ward, and I don't think many people have heard about it, either. But then everyone's talking about the wedding that's coming off soon.... Such an event for us all!" She appeared to brighten for a brief while. "Sir Peter has promised to send cars for us all. Such a very kind gentlemen!"

"Er—yes," Victoria answered.

"One doesn't meet many like him nowadays." Quite obviously she was against progress. "And him so very rich, too."

"Er—yes," Victoria murmured again.

The postmistress—who also maintained a kind of general shop—peered at her shortsightedly once more across her loaded counter.

"You look a little young to me," she remarked, "to be taking care of the child. But perhaps there's someone with you at the cottage?"

"No, no one," from Victoria.

The grizzled eyebrows swept upward again.

"But it's rather a lonely cottage, and the people who were there last thought it was very lonely. But then perhaps they'd been used to rather a gay life abroad.... And in any case, they had a car. I expect you've got a car?"

"No." Victoria shook her head as well.

"No car? Then you really are cut off! Unless Sir Peter—"

"Sir Peter's chauffeur will take us for occasional drives."

"I see."

But Victoria was not convinced that she did see, and as she and Johnny walked back to Alder Cottage—and now that she knew the name of it she decided that it was very suitable, since the garden sloped to a river—she couldn't help wondering how the rest of the district would react to the news that Sir Peter Wycherley, on the very eve of marriage with a highly suitable young woman, had burdened himself with a ward who could quite easily have been his own son.

And that set Victoria thinking along quite different lines. She was beginning to feel more and more amazed because Sir Peter had taken such a firm line about Johnny. She simply could not understand why he had had to do anything quite so drastic as the undertaking to look after Johnny for the rest of his adolescent life was likely to turn out to be. If he had children of his own there would almost certainly be awkwardness, and she was absolutely certain that Sir Peter's fiancée did not approve.

Hardly any young woman on the verge of marriage would.

But for the first time she wondered what the district would think, and how Sir Peter would explain away Johnny...and herself. Surely he was being a little rash in burdening himself with both of them? A young woman whom the postmistress thought looked very young, but was rather too young to be Johnny's mother.

Or was she?

She began to work it out for herself. Since Johnny was eight and she was twenty-two that really put her out of court as a mother for Johnny. But she wasn't quite sure that she wanted to be put out of court as a mother for Johnny. For some perverse reason she wasn't in the least sure, since Sir Peter was old enough—and more than old enough!—to be his father!

Lunch was a tremendous success because the up-to-the-minute stove in the kitchen worked beautifully. One would have had to be a very bad cook indeed to fail to produce something eatable after wading through the list of recipes in the cookbook that had been purchased with it, and hung beside it on the wall. Victoria was debating whether or not to send Johnny upstairs for a short nap when a woman who looked rather like the woman at the post office, but was actually much nicer, arrived at the side door and announced that she had been instructed by Sir Peter to present herself at the cottage for a few hours daily to do essential chores.

"Like scrubbing the kitchen floor, and things like that." She beamed at Victoria. "You don't look to me as if you're accustomed to scrubbing floors, my dear, and after all it isn't your job, is it? To look after the little lad is your job.''

Victoria felt somewhat taken aback.

"But it's such a tiny cottage—" she began.

Her new daily woman waved a hand and laughed.

"Don't you talk about tiny cottages, my dear." In the whole course of their association Victoria was to be addressed as "my dear" by Mrs. Wavertree. "They get dirty whether they're big or small, and in my experience the smaller they are the dirtier they get. Especially when there are youngsters running around."

But she seemed to take a great fancy to Johnny, and as she knew a lot about birds and he was beginning to take a serious interest in wildlife it seemed likely that they would get along very well. Also, there was no doubt about it. Mrs. Wavertree was prepared to revere him because he was Sir Peter's ward.

Or about to become Sir Peter's acknowledged responsibility.

Mrs. Wavertree gave the scrupulously clean kitchen what she called a going over, and would have performed the same function for the sitting room-living room, only Victoria had already cleaned it thoroughly that morning, and Mrs. Wavertree took her departure, promising to return the following day.

For the next few days the pattern of that first day at the cottage repeated itself, and Victoria and Johnny—with the assistance of Mrs. Wavertree—settled into a routine. In the mornings they rose early,

had their breakfast, walked to the village and did a
certain amount of shopping, and sometimes extended
their walk farther afield, returned to the cottage for
the preparation and consumption of their midday
meal. After that, the rest of the day was usually spent
in the garden, with Johnny chasing butterflies or dig-
ging in a small part of the garden that he had decided
to call his own, while Victoria got down to the serious
business of ridding the garden of weeds.

It was a forbidding task, and a backaching one,
but she enjoyed it. And more than anything else she
enjoyed reclaiming the borders and the various beds
that had once been devoted to flowers. She trimmed
the pocket-handerchief lawns and weeded the paths,
and within a week Alder Cottage was standing in the
midst of a very pleasant plot instead of being overrun
by suckers and thistles and the other enemies of order
in an enclosed piece of land. Even the orchard received some attention from her, and the hedges. She
could be seen going round with hedge clippers and
standing on step ladders and peering into the lane
while she shaped box hedges and beech hedges, and
cut back the buddleia so that the small white-painted
garden gate could be opened with ease and without a
shower of caterpillars descending on her head every
time she passed through it from the lane.

The lane, for some strange reason, fascinated her,
and she decided it was because it was so secret and
lonely, but on top of a step ladder anyone traveling
along it could be viewed from the moment they

rounded the bend which shut out the straight track to
the village. Also, on top of a step ladder, she felt, like
Johnny, as if she was in a position of great advantage, and no one could possibly take her unawares.

Not even Sir Peter Wycherley when he paid them
his next—or rather, first—visit.

But Sir Peter did not come anywhere near Alder
Cottage for a full fortnight after Victoria moved into
it with her charge. He had arranged for Mrs. Wavertree to keep a motherly eye on them and to take on
the major share of the housework, and from the local
farm dairy produce was delivered daily. The cottage
contained everything they could possibly need to insure their physical comfort, and on their third day at
the cottage Hawkins, Sir Peter's chauffeur, arrived
with a sleek gray Bentley outside the gate of the cottage, and indicated to Victoria that he was prepared
to take her anywhere she wished to go within reason.

By that he meant that if she wished to visit the
nearest town now was her opportunity, or if she
simply wished to go for a drive—accompanied, of
course, by Johnny—now was also her opportunity.

But Victoria, feeling strangely perverse, for some
reason she herself did not understand, resisted the
pull of Johnny's hand, and his eager importuning,
and told Hawkins she had no desire whatsoever to go
shopping on that particular day, and she was not
anxious, either to be taken for a drive. To the surprise of Hawkins she dismissed him with a sweet
smile and an air of being perfectly content where she

was, and to Johnny's mortification and acute disappointment the Bentley rolled away, and the two of
them stood watching it until the curve in the lane had
taken it out of sight.

After Hawkins had driven away Victoria was so
sorry for Johnny that she offered to take him for a
long walk, if that would suffice, or on a visit to the
post office where he could buy one of several items
that appealed to him every time they entered it for
other purposes. But Johnny, dazzled by the shine of
the Bentley, and already developing tastes that were
no doubt quite all right in his case, since he was to
become Sir Peter's official ward, refused to be com-
pensated for missing the ride in the Bentley, and
actually took himself off and sulked.

Victoria was surprised, but not unsympathetic.
After all, almost any child would have preferred a
ride in the Bentley to the promise of a box of colored
pencils or a plastic farm tractor. But Johnny had not
always enjoyed these amenities, and she was considerably amazed that he had assimilated luxury quite so
quickly.

For his sake she hoped that everything went well in
the future, and there were no hitches in connection
with his adoption papers. So far nothing was really
official, and she had been brought up to accept that
there is many a slip between the cup and the lip.

But Johnny was not the type who sulked for long,
and within a matter of half an hour he had regained
his usual sunny humor. Victoria baked him a choco-

late cake for his tea, and by the time tea was over the
Bentley was forgotten, and the farm tractor preoccupied him completely.

The next day passed without incident and in a completely unruffled manner, and the day after that was
just as placidly pleasant. Victoria wondered whether
Peter Wycherley had forgotten them, and then she
decided he was far too preoccupied to have time for
their existence. After all, an engaged man must have
many things to make demands on his time, and an
engaged man who was planning to marry quite soon
must have quite a number of things to do.

She began to get a little short of ready cash, and
she decided that she would have to draw something
out of her post office account. She hesitated to touch
the tiny balance that she had in an ordinary bank.
She had been spending her own money for food and
other essentials, and housekeeping was making serious inroads on her resources.

Not that that worried her, for she had been prepared to maintain Johnny entirely without outside
assistance. But she did think it a little curious that Sir
Peter, who had been so emphatic about his intentions
toward Johnny, should have forgotten that in order
to exist at all one had to have the means to defray expenses, and a roof over their heads and extremely
comfortable surroundings were not really sufficient
to insure a high standard of living.

Neither was the daily contribution Mrs. Wavertree
made to their comfort.

However, for herself she was content, and more than content. She was living a kind of twilight existence that was hardly real; and certainly, the evenings after supper that she spent walking up and down on the flagged path before the cottage in the moonlight, watching the bats flitting to and fro in the dusk and listening for sounds on the white road beyond the garden gate, inhaling the perfume of the honeysuckle, were scarcely real at all.

She couldn't get away from a strange, unaccountable feeling of excitement.

CHAPTER TEN

SHE WAS WALKING up and down in the moonlight when she heard the car coming along the road from the opposite direction to that in which lay the village.

It wasn't merely a moonlight night; it was a night of surpassing and quite extraordinary beauty. There was a faint haze rising from the fields surrounding the cottage, and the rays of the moon appeared to be imprisoned by the haze...caught up in it, as it were, and softened by it, so that the moonlight had a strange iridescent quality, and fell as gently as a caress.

The tobacco plant was smelling strongly, and so was the night-scented stock. As for the honeysuckle, it was like a background to Victoria's thoughts, a challenge to her blood. She felt her blood quicken and leap along her veins when she inhaled the perfume of the cascades of honeysuckle that clothed the garden wall.

She had known little or nothing in the way of romance, and yet romance seemed in the very air she breathed. And it was more than romance. It was magic.

She felt a strange yearning to share it with someone.

The sound of the car was just a fat kiss of tires on the surface of the road when she first heard it. And then there was silence as it slid to a standstill outside the gate, and then the gate clicked open and footsteps approached along the garden path.

The footsteps sounded hollow in the silence of the night, and for a second or so Victoria was alarmed . . . alarmed because she could see no one, and the growth was thick at each side of the garden path. And then a figure emerged and stood in the moonlight confronting her, and she recognized her visitor immediately, despite the fact that he was wearing full evening dress.

He was obviously quite real, although at first she thought he was a figment of her imagination, and he looked as if he had deserted some important social gathering in a hurry, and was not quite sure of his reception. He looked at her with curious diffidence.

"I hope I didn't startle you," he said.

During her brief moment of panic her hands had gone up to her face, but she lowered them in a relaxed manner as she answered his query.

"No," she said, not altogether truthfully.

He was staring at her. She was wearing a light blue dress, and because of the warmth of the night she was not even wearing a cardigan over it. Her pale gold hair was full of moonbeams, and her complexion was extraordinarily clear, and as pale as a moonbeam. More jerkily he spoke.

"You look like a sprite," he said.

Victoria smiled.

"It's the night. It's a wonderful night, isn't it?"

"Beautiful."

"Nothing is quite real on a night like this. I . . . You—you look as if you oughtn't to be here."

"As a matter of fact, I oughtn't." He shrugged. "But after all, I'm still a free agent."

"Meaning that you're not yet—not yet a married man?"

"Something like that."

The diamond stud in the front of his shirt winked at her. She marveled at the utter impeccableness of his linen, and was intrigued by the dark silk handkerchief tucked in at the end of his sleeve.

"Would you—would you like to go inside?"

She was not at all sure why all at once she felt so diffident and hesitant in his presence, but she did. Also she felt peculiarly impressed by him, even slightly fascinated by his beautifully shaved appearance and the gentle shimmer on his hair.

He was a most attractive man, and apparently he hadn't entirely forgotten her after all. Also—and for some reason she was quite sure about this—he looked upset.

His gray eyes gazed at her almost broodingly.

"Not unless you want to go inside." He fell into step beside her as she moved along the path. "Do you make a habit of standing out here at this time of night and simply admiring the night?"

"Yes." She smiled up at him. "The weather has been perfectly marvelous for the last fortnight, and I absolutely adore this garden—and this time of day. I simply couldn't go quietly up to bed while it's all so magical out here."

"Go to bed?" He glanced at his watch as they crossed the pocket-handkerchief lawn in the direction of a white-painted garden seat that had been placed beneath another buddleia tree. "But it's not yet ten o'clock! Surely you don't go to bed before ten on a summer evening?"

She shrugged.

"If it hadn't been a fine night I would have been in bed," she admitted. "What else is there to do in the country when you haven't even a television set to watch?"

Instantly he started apologizing.

"I'm so sorry. I said I would do something about television, didn't I? And a transistor radio for Johnny. This is all very remiss of me! I'm afraid I've been somewhat preoccupied. You'll just have to forgive me!"

"It's perfectly all right," Victoria assured him. She was ashamed of herself now that she had even mentioned such a thing as a television set when he had so kindly provided them with a roof over their heads. "I only said that because you asked me why I didn't sit up late...and I do sometimes, as a matter of fact. On a night like this I like to roam about in the garden, and that's much nicer than watching television. Much nicer than doing a lot of things!"

They had reached the white-painted garden seat, and he waited until she had dropped down on it before taking his place beside her. And he looked worried all at once.

"I'm not sure I approve of that," he told her, his gray eyes plainly obviously intrigued by her slim blue shape in the moonlight. "After all, this is a lonely spot"—he glanced around him, as if aware for the first time of how extremely lonely and definitely cut off it was—"and there's no near neighbor, or anyone like that. Considering that there are only the two of you here—and one is upstairs in bed from about six o'clock onwards—I do earnestly feel that I ought to advise you not to roam about out here in the garden when it's as late as this. Why, you never know what might happen!"

She smiled.

"I'm not afraid."

"But you looked afraid when I came along the path just now! Just before you recognized me you looked as if you were contemplating bolting into the house and turning the key upon me!

Victoria had to admit that for one moment the advisability of such an undignified course as that had crossed her mind—until she had recognized him.

"And yet you tell me you're not afraid."

"Well, shall we say I'm not often afraid!"

He lay back against the garden seat and she received the distinct impression that he was relaxing... quite possibly for the first time that day. He looked up into the branches of the buddleia tree, caught a glimpse of the stars, rendered hazy by the moonlight and the faint vapor rising from the fields and the woods, and if she had been asked to give a description of his expression all at once she would have described it as extraordinarily peaceful and content. He even sighed a little.

"Well, I must say that I envy you living here," he confessed surprisingly. "It's a different world from the one I've been inhabiting all day. An enchanted world!"

Although he had not so far apologized for neglecting them—her and Johnny—she felt appeased by this tribute. For she felt precisely the same about Alder Cottage and its surroundings herself, which seemed to indicate they were on a similar sort of wavelength.

"But Wycherley Park is a very attractive place," she reminded him. "Your gardens are beautifully laid out and cared for, and wandering in them in the evenings is delightful, as I had an opportunity to find out for myself."

"Did you?" He glanced at her almost sharply.

"Well, you know you provided me with sanctuary for quite a while."

"But it wasn't the same as this, was it?" He leaned a little toward her, insisting on finding out whether she really agreed with him. "I mean, here it is different!"

"It's very much more humble, and, as you say, cut off."

"But a young woman like you should simply loathe being cut off from the world."

"Well, I don't."

He sighed again, as if he could hardly believe her, but it was pleasant to hear such an admission if it was really true. Half wonderingly he observed, as his gray eyes roved over her:

"Well, you certainly look as if you belong here... half woman, half vaporous creature of moonlight and magic." His eyes smiled at her lazily. "I find you very peaceful, Victoria of Alder Cottage! Does Johnny like it here, too?"

"I'm sure he loves it here."

"Good." He had recently lighted a fresh cigarette, and the fragrance of the tobacco in some curious way acutely emphasized the fragrance of the nicotine. "I'm sorry if I appeared to have forgotten your joint existences, but I've had a lot of things to think about... a great deal on my mind."

"Don't apologize," she said dryly. "An engaged man must have many things to think about."

"Ah, but you see I'm no longer engaged!" He ran the fingers of one well-shaped hand through the trim orderliness of his hair, ruffling it considerably and destroying the satinlike shimmer. "At least, I don't think I am! I walked out on the lady concerned about an hour and a half ago, and she told me I need make no effort to contact her again. I suppose you could interpret that as a broken engagement.''

"Oh, but I am sorry! I'm really very sorry!" Victoria certainly sounded as if she was appalled by the thought of his world lying in fragments at his feet; but in all honesty she had to admit to herself—despite her conviction that he must be really terribly upset—he didn't look like a man who was reeling under the effects of a major disaster. He didn't even look like a man who was afflicted by the effects of a disaster at all.

Just a little bit perturbed—almost whimsically concerned, she would have said, if she had been asked. Slightly bewildered, perhaps mildly hurt. But not shattered, not stunned.

"That's very kind of you." He crossed one long leg over the other, and looked upward into the branches. "Very kind. But engagements have been broken before, you know."

"Yes; but when it happens to you personally...I mean, it probably isn't anything very serious. You'll make it up again."

"Will I?" and he glanced at her whimsically.

"I hope so. Otherwise you're going to be very unhappy."

"That's a possibility, of course."

"You mean that you'll make it up?"

"No, that I'll be very unhappy...for a time, at least."

But he was smiling in such a way that she still

couldn't believe he fully realized what it was that had happened to him. Perhaps it was a case of delayed shock. Perhaps he was already planning to make it up, and therefore the whole incident wasn't regarded by him as very serious.

"What happened?" she inquired, hoping he would not think her impertinent. "Of course," hurriedly, "if you don't think you ought to discuss the matter...."

"Oh, but I do," he assured her. "I do because it was largely because of you—and Johnny, of course—that my plans have been somewhat rudely upset. Listen!" He held up a finger. "Isn't that a nightingale singing in that coppice over there? In the whole course of my life so far there have been few occasions when a bird with a throat like that has suddenly made up its mind to entertain me. But I should think there can be hardly any doubt that that is a nightingale."

But Victoria was appalled.

"You mean you've broken off your engagement because of me?" she demanded. "And Johnny?"

His gray eyes gleamed at her in an amused manner.

"Oh, I didn't break off the engagement. It was the lady who did that," he corrected any false impression she might have received.

"B-but because of—Johnny and me?"

"Largely, I'd say, because of you and Johnny." He sat listening with a rapt look on his face to the nightingale's outpourings. "No wonder you enjoy sitting out here in the garden if you can listen to that sort of thing," he commented.

"I—I don't quite understand why Johnny and I should have played any part in your broken engagement," she told him. "I mean, you didn't have to adopt Johnny. Not if Miss Islesworth was so strongly against it."

"She wasn't so violently opposed to my adopting Johnny as she was to my retaining you to look after him," he admitted.

"Oh, but that—that's terrible!"

He patted her knee.

"Don't let it upset you. You and Johnny are indivisible, and I pointed it out."

"We don't have to indivisible. In any case, you could have just let us go—"

"I didn't choose to let you go. Now, let's devote five peaceful seconds to listening to that bird!"

At the end of the five seconds Victoria felt she had to make it clear to him that he had startled and perturbed her. After all, if she was to be the cause of ruining his life.... Well, it was unthinkable. Something would have to be done about it quickly.

"What happened?" she asked again. "If you won't think me rude for demanding to know! After all, if it concerns me so closely I ought to know, and then I can do my best to put matters right. Sir Peter," as he sat there smiling at her in that strange, placid fashion, "you must surely understand that to be the cause of interfering with a couple's marriage plans is a most serious thing. I wouldn't have had anything like this happen for the world if I could have prevented it.''

"I'm sure you wouldn't," he agreed.

"And as I'm the unwitting cause of all the trouble I feel all the more strongly about it!''

"Don't worry," he said again, with that hint of complacency in his tone. "I'm not going to shoot myself, or anything like that. I may make an attempt tomorrow to patch things up.''

"Why not tonight?''

"Because Georgina's in a very difficult humor tonight.''

"I'm not surprised if you walked out on her.''

He shrugged.

"I didn't exactly walk out on her. She flounced out on me! We were going out to dinner—rather an important dinner, as a matter of fact—and I called to collect her at her father's house. It's about a couple of miles the other side of Wycherley Park. The two estates will march well together one of these days, or so her father seems to think.''

"Never mind about the estates. What started the quarrel?''

"She asked me where I had hidden you and Johnny, and I told her.''

"Oh!''

"She made some unpleasant reference to secret love-nests, and I'm afraid I lost my temper. The argument was short, sharp, and bitter, and then I told her I hadn't any appetite for dinner. She flew upstairs to her room and left me standing in the hall of her father's house with no one to talk to save the butler, who looked horrified by what he had over-heard, and I said good night to him politely and walked out of the house and got into my car and came here.''

''Oh!'' Victoria said again.

''And here we are sitting on the lawn and listening to your nightingale, and I think you're beginning to shiver, so we ought to go indoors.'' His gray eyes watched her in a concerned fashion. ''You did shiver, didn't you?''

Victoria shook her head.

''No. It's just that I—I feel so horribly guilty....''

''Silly child,'' he said gently, and placed his hand beneath her elbow and urged her to her feet. ''We can't have you catching pneumonia,'' he remarked. ''Besides, the light looks cozy in the cottage. I'd like to go inside and see what you've done to the place.''

''At this time of night?'' She sounded almost hor-rified, particularly as the words 'love-nest' were echoing inside her head in a most unpleasant manner; and although it was quite ridiculous, of course, that Miss Islesworth should have so far forgotten her own dignity as to accuse him—a man like Sir Peter Wycherley, who must impress most people as being entirely unlike the type who went in for love-nests—of a peculiarly distasteful form of unfaithfulness was so horrible, particularly as it involved herself, that she quite shrank from letting him into the cottage.

He frowned down at her suddenly with displeasure.

"Silly child," he said more forcefully. "If you imagine I take any notice of what a jealous woman says you must be mad. And you certainly don't know me! If you were not here to look after Johnny I would find someone else to look after him...it's as simple and uncomplicated as that! Do you understand what I mean? And now will you let me into the cottage?"

She nodded. He could not have put it more clearly that, whatever his ex-fiancée thought, he himself was so little aware of Miss Victoria Wood apart from her usefulness and her value because of her obvious devotion to Johnny—as a young person who could intrigue him or make his admittance into her cottage (which was actually his) at close upon eleven o'clock at night. He didn't view this as any sort of a menace to her reputation or her future prospects that it was almost an insult to her own young womanhood.

As he smiled down at her a little coolly out of those quiet gray eyes of his, she gathered that he was not merely indifferent to her, but he was completely indifferent.

"I—I—" she stammered. "I merely thought that it was a little late...."

"But you do realize that I've driven quite a long way to see you? And I want to hear about Johnny! I want to find out how you've been managing with your housekeeping, and I want to give you a check—"

At that she protested violently.

"I don't need money!"

"All the same, I mean to make a small sum over to you." He opened the door of the cottage, and they walked straight into the living room, where the grandfather clock was ticking at the foot of the stairs. He glanced around him with a look of appreciation on his face as the mellow light in the living room revealed the bowl of roses on the gate-legged table, and another big bowl of flowers on the highly polished sideboard. The small, enclosed space was sweet with the scent of flowers and beeswax, and it also had a lived-in, distinctly 'homely' look with Victoria's knitting lying in the middle of the couch, and the book she had been reading flung down on a small occasional table.

She had been having a cup of coffee before she went out into the garden, and her coffee cup was standing beside her book. There was also a small book in which she had been totting up her expenditure on food and so forth.

Sir Peter walked across to her novel and picked it up and looked at it, but he did not touch her accounts-book. Instead he went across to the desk and sat down at it, then drew out a check book from his pocket and a handsome gold pen.

"How much of your own money have you been spending?" he asked.

"Not much."

"Then you and Johnny have been living on air?"

"Of course not," she denied.

He wrote his check and handed it over to her.

"You can cash that at the local bank, or pay it into your own account as you think fit. I have added a couple of months' salary to the amount I estimate you will require for housekeeping, and if you find you need more you can always ask for it."

He tilted back in his chair and smiled a little peculiarly as he handed over the check.

Victoria started to protest instantly when she saw the amount of the check. Not merely did it mean she was to receive a very, very generous salary, but it meant she and Johnny were to cost him far more than they were either of them worth—certainly to him, at the present time! Altogether, it was far too much money to receive from a man who didn't need to act the part of their mutual benefactor, and she told him so.

"I realize that you want Johnny to have everything you consider he should have, but this is far, far too much!"

He got up leisurely from the desk and went across to her. He placed his hands on her shoulders.

"Miss Victoria Wood," he told her solemnly, "I honestly believe you would look a gift horse in the mouth!"

She flushed.

"I haven't any right to receive a gift horse."

"I've told you somebody has to be the recipient of this particular gift horse, so why do you object? It simply means that you are now on my payroll—like Hawkins and the rest!"

She flushed more brilliantly while the light beat down upon her.

"You relieve my mind of a burden of anxiety," she declared breathlessly.

"Do I?"

There was no expression on his face, but his eyes were cool.

"In that case you're rather a foolish young woman!"

Then she felt his fingers biting into the soft flesh of her shoulders, and for one moment she thought he was actually angry with her.

"Did you never make a mistake yourself?" he asked, in a carefully controlled manner.

She looked up at him in bewilderment.

"A mistake—?"

"A serious mistake." He laid one finger lightly on the gold of her hair, and then he let her go. "It's too late for riddles, isn't it, so I'll let you go to bed. But you can tell Johnny I shall be seeing him quite soon, and you can buy him something he wants out of that check." He moved regretfully toward the door. "This cottage has always appealed to me, and now I find it has a strange attraction." He turned his head and looked at her over his shoulder.

For the first time she realized that his eyes were

telling her something...or trying to tell her something. "Good-night, Victoria...I'm going to stop calling you Miss Wood. If nightingales can sing for you and Johnny has adopted you I certainly am not going to behave toward you as if you had all the dignity of an ordinary young woman. You are not an ordinary young woman.... You are very far from being anything of the kind. And tonight I am free and I can say what I like, and I would like you to know that I—consider you fit in beautifully here at the cottage!"

He smiled at her a little crookedly.

"When I see you again I shall probably not be free, so if you insist on formality I will then address you as Miss Wood. And we shall remain Miss Wood and Sir Peter Wycherley for the remainder of our lives! But tonight you are Victoria!"

She moved nearer to him as he opened to door.

"Good-night, Sir Peter," she said quietly.

One of his eyebrows ascended.

"What, if I condescend to address you as Victoria won't you return the compliment by addressing me as Peter? Just for one night! Tomorrow, I assure you, I shall be an engaged man again, and I don't think my fiancée would like it if you called me Peter. So...just for tonight! Because we listened to that nightingale together?"

He took her hand, and she let it lie in his warm brown clasp, and she lifted her eyes to his and obediently said what he wanted her to say:

"Good-night, Peter. And—and thank you!"

"For what?"

He smiled still more crookedly, gave her back her hand, glanced rapidly round the living room, and then strode out into the waning moonlight.

She listened to his firm footsteps walking down the garden path to the gate, and it was not until she heard his car starting up —or thought she heard it starting up—that she closed the door.

But he came hurrying back.

"Lock it, Victoria," he ordered. "Lock it and bolt it, do you understand? And make sure all your windows are fastened, and—"

"But I can't sleep with a closed window," she told him breathlessly.

"Then stay awake with a securely snibbed one! This cottage is far too lonely!" He frowned at her before he himself shut the door, and he waited for her to drive home the bolts. Then he called from outside:

"Good-night!"

She called back with a wild feeling of excitement rendering her voice a trifle husky.

"Good-night!"

CHAPTER ELEVEN

THE NEXT MORNING he was back with his arms full of parcels and the Bentley left standing in the road in close proximity to the garden gate.

It was barely eight o'clock, and the kitchen of the cottage was full of the smell of burning toast—which Victoria, most unfortunately, had temporarily forgotten—coffee and scrambled eggs. Johnny was sitting at the table and disposing of a bowl of cereal laced with cream, and Victoria was tying an apron about her slender middle and wondering whether she dared add another rasher to the ones that were sizzling in the pan for her own consumption as well as Johnny's, or whether it would be wiser to stick to her normal diet of toast and marmalade.

Both Victoria and Johnny heard the car stop outside the gate, and Johnny let forth a jubilant whoop because he thought it was Hawkins returned to place himself at their disposal for the day. But Victoria recognized the footsteps as soon as she heard them echoing on the flagged path which continued round an angle of the house until it ended up at the kitchen door; and as the kitchen door was standing open to admit the sunshine she was the first to have her suspicions confirmed and to welcome the owner of the cottage when he stood smiling at them somewhat broadly from the sweetness of the morning outside.

"I hope I'm not interrupting your breakfast," he said. "But I'll admit I hoped you would offer me some coffee as I haven't had any breakfast myself yet."

He deposited his parcels on a side table, then stood sniffing the atmosphere appreciatively.

"Burnt toast! Do you know, I have a weakness for it! Do you think you could spare me a piece?" And he actually robbed the toast rack of one of its most highly carbonized exhibits and proceeded to munch it with appetite.

He sat down on the arm of a chair and winked at Johnny.

"Have a look at my parcels," he said. "There are one or two things among them that might interest you."

While Johnny rushed at the parcels Victoria hastily set another place at the table for their unexpected visitor, and then attempted to deprive him of the remains of his burnt toast.

"You can't possibly eat that," she declared. "It's practically black! For goodness' sake, if you're hungry, sit down and have a proper breakfast."

He grinned at her. His teeth were amazingly white in the strong sunshine, and although it was so early in the morning and it had been fairly late when he left the cottage the night before he was beautifully shaved and impeccably groomed as always.

"Thank you, that's what I mean to do," he told her. He pulled out his own chair at the table and sat down while she was still frantically calculating whether she had enough sausages and bacon in the refrigerator to provide him with a really substantial breakfast. His voice dropped to a lower key, and was suddenly very soft. "Don't tell me I'm not welcome?"

"Of course." She hardly knew what she was saying, and for some reason she felt quite ridiculously confused. She was also having the strange experience of someone who was making new discoveries...how indolent his gray eyes were, and yet how attractively bright. His eyelashes were far too long and thick to be the possession of a mere man, and when he smiled his eyes crinkled up at the corners and he appeared to be studying her through the fringes of his eyelashes. His mouth was exceptionally shapely, and his chin reassuringly square. There was a brightness about his hair, and yet in patches it was very dark—dark as a blackbird's plumage.

"Well?" As she stood there looking down at him as if something about him had had a stupefying effect on her senses he smiled in a somewhat peculiar manner. "Am I welcome? Or would you rather I went?"

"No, no, no!" In her eagerness to convince him she actually laid a hand on his shoulder. "Of course I don't want you to go. I mean—"

"Splendid." The softness—it could even have been a caressing note—was back in his voice again, and a completely relaxed look overspread his features. "Then I'll stay."

As Johnny danced about the kitchen delightedly with a new transistor radio swinging from one hand and a beautifully bound book on butterflies held aloft in the other, Victoria dived into the larder, and when she reappeared Sir Peter was helping himself to cornflakes. Johnny poured cream over them for him.

"We always have breakfast in the kitchen," Victoria apologized, still not quite certain what she was saying, or why she was saying it.

"And why not?" Certainly the check cloth was very bright, and the flowers in the small Wedgwood jar in the middle of it a gay and attractive centerpiece. "It reminds me of my nursery days."

She glanced at him.

"I didn't expect to see you this morning. I—I imagined you would have other things to do."

"Such as?"

He was buttering a roll while she slid some more slices of bread under the grill.

She flushed. He had lifted his eyes to her and they were dancing with amusement. Despite Johnny's presence he persisted in attempting to elicit from her what she thought he should have been doing instead of paying another visit to the cottage.

"Are you rather inclined to the opinion that the very first thing I should have done this morning is get in touch with a certain person by telephone and offer her my abject apologies? Because if that's what you really think I should have done I'm afraid I have to disappoint you.''

"You mean you didn't telephone?''

"I didn't even send a hurried note round by Hawkins saying how very sorry I am for everything.''

"But . . . .'' She prodded a sausage that was sizzling in the pan, and he asked politely if he couldn't have two sausages—three if she could manage it. "You can't mean that you—that you don't intend to—to—''

"At the moment I'm free, and I'm enjoying my freedom. It's because I'm free that I'm here. Didn't I say to you last night that so long as I was free—''

Johnny interrupted with a wide-eyed look.

"I didn't know you were here last night!''

His guardian dismissed him amiably.

"If you've finished your breakfast, old chap, do go outside and get some fresh air. You can polish up the car for me if you like. I'm sure Victoria's got a duster in the drawer.''

Johnny was enchanted by the notion, and departed, taking his transistor with him. Victoria placed a heaped plateful of eggs, bacon, sausages and mushrooms in front of Sir Peter, and then stood looking down at him a trifle censoriously.

"Last night,'' she reminded him, "you said I was to call you Peter because today you were going to do the right thing and apologize to Miss Islesworth and make everything up with her. You assured me that after last night everything would be as it was again.''

"And that was why I wanted to hear you call me Peter?''

"Y-yes.''

"A condemned man's last request before sentence was carried out!''

"I—I don't understand you!''

She sat down at the kitchen table, and while he applied himself to his breakfast in a businesslike fashion—ever afterward she was to hold the belief very close to her heart that unless an Englishman is fed he is unapproachable—she played with the butter knife and watched him. He occasionally smiled at her in a detached manner, and finally agreed that they would discuss the problem later on.

"But for the time being I'm feeling too replete. Your cooking is excellent, Victoria.''

"You mean that you—you're going to stay here?''

"I'm not going back immediately. As a matter of fact, I thought we'd have another picnic today—as it's such a fine day. Would you like to pay another visit to the spot where we had our other picnic?''

"I—But do you think you ought to waste the time?''

"You forget that Johnny is my ward, and nothing is wasted on him. But wouldn't you like it yourself?''

She carefully avoided his eyes, for the simple reason that this morning she didn't dare to meet them fully. . . or at any rate, not for long.

"Of course I'd like it. But you have other things to do!"

"The 'other things' can wait."

For an instant she did meet his eyes, and to her astonishment the gray depths were pleading with her.

"Victoria." He laid his hand over hers where it rested on the tablecloth. "Victoria, I want to forget everything today—everything but the things I wish particularly to remember. And among the things I wish to remember are the way you looked last night and the extraordinary effect moonlight has on your hair. Victoria!" He bent nearer to her, and she caught the fragrance of his shaving lotion. "Victoria," a trifle huskily, "it's such an absurdly formal name for such a scrap of informal young womanhood, but in my ears it has acquired a certain music. Will you take compassion on the condemned man today and accompany him back to that green bank where we disported ourselves before, and where Johnny ate so many sausage rolls and cheese straws and drank so much ginger pop that I thought he'd explode in the car when he got back into it? Will you, Victoria?"

She said breathlessly:

"My father used to call me Vicky."

"I still prefer Victoria!"

"And you did say that after last night—"

"Forget what I said last night. Let's go to the river, Victoria!"

She rose, half laughing, half protesting still.

"But what about food?"

"I have it in the car. Another hamper for the special delight of Johnny. How long will it take you to wash up? Or can you leave these things on the table as they are?"

"No, no, I'll clear everything away and tidy up before we leave."

"I thought you'd say that."

"This doesn't happen to be Mrs. Wavertree's day."

He smiled at her and she smiled back. For the first time she felt as if she had known him for the whole of her life.

"I'll wait outside," he said.

In the road beyond the garden gate Johnny was working hard. With a yellow duster and a great deal of elbow grease he was achieving miracles...although it was true the car had looked very bright and shining to start with.

When he heard about the picnic Johnny reacted, as always, in a completely normal manner. He wanted to start off immediately, but Victoria insisted on completing her normal round of housework before slipping into a cool, clean cotton dress that was an enchanting shade of apple-blossom pink and declaring she was ready to lock up the cottage.

Sir Peter looked at her, long and hard, as she turned the front door key, and he seemed to have some difficulty on concentrating on driving when they set off. Johnny had insisted on occupying the seat beside him at the wheel, and that meant that Victoria was once more relegated to the back, which didn't seem to please Sir Peter at all.

"I do think, Johnny," he said, "that you should allow a lady to exercise the power of choice. For all you know to the contrary Victoria may dislike sitting alone in the back of the car, and I may dislike having a small boy bouncing about in the seat beside me. Quite honestly, if I could choose, I'd prefer to have Victoria sitting beside me."

Johnny instantly looked dashed.

"But you said you'd teach me to drive a car—"

"One day I will," his guardian promised. "But at the moment you're far too small."

Victoria protested from the back of the car.

"I'm perfectly comfortable where I am."

But Sir Peter spoke inflexibly.

"Change over, Johnny. If you behave in an exceptionally exemplary manner I may allow you to sit beside me on the way home." His expression was amiable, but that note in his voice was not to be ignored. Johnny executed the change without even a protest, and Victoria landed in the seat beside the driver. But she thought it necessary to continue her protest.

"Poor Johnny! If you knew what a very great treat it is for him to sit beside you!" she said indignantly.

Sir Peter glanced at her sideways and smiled a little peculiarly.

"I like to have a young thing in pink sitting beside

me,'' he remarked. "By the way, you should wear it
more often...although I think, when you're sitting
in the moonlight, blue is the color for you. That
nightingale last night obviously agreed with me.''

Victoria said nothing, but she was beginning to feel
a trifle self-conscious...in fact, rather more than a
trifle self-conscious. And despite Johnny's disappointment she felt suddenly almost as excited as she
had felt for a brief while the night before. Quite
unreasonably excited, of course.

They took the same route to the river that they had
taken before, and when they reached it they followed
the same procedure as before. The hamper was un-
packed, the contents disposed of, and after that
Johnny wandered away and left his two elders. While
he hunted for frogs instead of butterflies this time
Victoria repacked the hamper and Sir Peter packed a
pipe with tobacco and looked along the stem of it
thoughtfully before applying a match.

He had done this on the previous occasion, but he
had done it while he was lying flat on his back and
displaying every intention of enjoying a short nap.
But on this occasion there was no drowsiness in his
eyes, and there was certainly no evidence of drowsiness in Victoria's...so he lowered his pipe and
reached over and took the damask tablecloth away
from her and flung it carelessly aside on the bank
before he pulled her to her feet.

"Why should Johnny be the only active one
among us?'' he asked. "Let's explore the woods.''

Victoria followed him into the woods, and obediently halted when he halted, and continued when he advanced. It was really far too hot for constant movement, and when they reached a kind of clearing where the ground was soft with pine needles and the rays of the sun were excluded by a lacy canopy overhead Sir Peter once more took the initiative and flung his coat on the ground for Victoria to sit on.

She was about to protest—and she had done a lot of protesting that day so far—that the pine needles were soft and inviting enough without his coat when she accidentally stumbled, and he caught her and held her for fully twenty seconds before they both realized that it was a somewhat unconventional pose. Victoria detached herself with primness and sank down on the pine needles, feeling a little breathless as he folded up his coat.

"So you decline to sit on it?" he said. "You're an obstinate young thing, Victoria!"

They talked—both of them making an obvious effort at first—about all sorts of things they had never discussed before, and Victoria learned a good deal of his boyhood and his parents and his general background, while he heard about her parents and the comparatively lonely, and certainly insecure, life she had led since she was deprived of them.

"And instead of doing the sensible thing and taking a sensible job with prospects you attempt to burden yourself with Johnny," he said censoriously. "You must be mad!"

She shook her head.

"I don't think so. You see, Johnny hasn't anyone and I haven't anyone."

"He has now."

"Yes; he has you...."

"You say that as if you consider me a dubious acquisition."

She turned and looked at him, and in her harebell blue eyes he detected a certain amount of consternation because that wasn't what she had meant at all. What she had meant was that he wasn't free to attach himself to Johnny, and in the interests of fairness Miss Islesworth had every right to object to him making the effort.

"How you will insist on dragging in Georgina," he observed with a frown, as he leaned on one elbow and lighted himself a cigarette.

"But she has to be dragged in," she insisted.

"She doesn't. Because I'm not going to marry her."

"You're—not going to—marry her?"

"That was what I said."

"But—"

"How full of buts you are!" He ground out the cigarette he had only just lighted, taking care it should not in its turn ignite the pine needles, and sat up and leaned toward her. He possessed himself of one of her hands, and while he examined the delicate fingernails and the insides of her slender wrists he told her somewhat jerkily why it was that he pro-

posed terminating his association with Miss Islesworth. In actual fact, he did more than that. He
accused her of breaking it up.

"That night you and Johnny turned up like a couple of waifs at the Park I knew that it had to end. The
reason that it had become an established fact had
ceased to exist! Before you came, Victoria," bending
her knuckles very slightly and gently, "my only interests were Wycherley and what was best for Wycherley, and that meant marriage and a suitable wife.
Georgina, from most people's point of view, I suppose, would make me a very suitable wife, and
although she's not in the least in love with me she
does love the country and all that goes to make up a
country way of life. In a way I admire her tremendously, and I'm lost in admiration when I see her on
a horse, and that sort of thing...but I've never had
the smallest illusion about how much I love her, or
how lost I'd feel if I had to do without her."

Victoria attempted to interrupt again, but he held
up a lean brown forefinger.

"No! Not until I've said my piece and made everything clear!" He fumbled automatically for his
cigarette case, then realized that he had just dis-
carded one, and put it away again. "The night you
and Johnny arrived we had been celebrating our engagement with a party. There were only a few of our
special friends, but they were the ones who had been
awaiting our engagement for a long time. Some of
them no doubt thought I'd been a bit tardy in putting

the question, but they couldn't possibly know that even I, fairly prosaic chap that I am, had had my dreams occasionally.''

He smiled a little twistedly, and his gray eyes forced Victoria's to meet them.

"When I was twenty-one I dreamed quite a lot. and my dreams always had something to do with a slip of a girl like you—one for whom the nightingales would sing even if they wouldn't sing for other people, and who had moonbeams in her hair when there wasn't even a gleam of moonlight! That night of the accident, when Johnny was deprived of his father and I had suddenly become officially pledged to marry someone, you turned up out of the night and I simply couldn't believe that you were real. Then, when it got through to me that you were real enough, it also got through to me that I was no longer free. I had been just that little bit too precipitate. So I thought up the next best thing to keep you near me. I decided to adopt Johnny, and as you were so attached to him I counted upon you being eager to stay and take charge of him...at any rate for a time. When that time had expired I suppose I understood perfectly that I would have to let you go.''

"And what about me?" Victoria asked, so quietly that it was almost a whisper in the warmth of the afternoon. "What about me? Or didn't I really count at all?''

He dropped her hand and put his fingers under her

chin, lifting it. He looked deep into the harebell blue eyes.

"What about you? Well, the only thing happened that could happen. I succeeded in freeing myself, and now I'm going to marry you!"

"Instead of Miss Islesworth?"

"Well, obviously, I don't intend to marry both of you."

"But you're not free!" She spoke insistently. "You can't say that just having a quarrel and walking out instead of staying to dinner is being released from an engagement! For one thing, she hasn't officially released you, has she?"

"I told you it was she who flounced out on me, and then I left. She said some very unpleasant things about you. . .and I left!"

She was looking up at him very earnestly, and although her pulses were behaving most eccentrically and her heart was hammering away like a wild thing seeking to burst forth from a cage, the obstinate streak in her nature would not allow her to accept the easy way out and acknowledge that he really was free. How could he be free, unless Georgina Islesworth didn't want to marry him after all?

"But she doesn't," he assured her, stroking one side of her cheek in a somewhat unsteady manner. His eyes were pleading with her, eager but a little apprehensive at the same time. "She actually told me I could go to you in some sort of love-nest, and that the whole district was talking. I told her I didn't care how much it talked, and that even if she didn't realize it I had long since admitted the fact to myself that she and I were not suited to one another. I said that if she had serious suspicions about you—which I declined to refute—she was as free as air to marry someone else, and she took my ring off and flung it on the floor at my feet, and said that she would be very happy indeed to be released.

"This morning I sent her back the ring with a note urging her to keep it, but I told her quite plainly that I considered myself to be absolved from all obligation to marry her. In fact, I told her that I was going to marry you . . . if you would have me!" with sudden humbleness.

But still Victoria could not reach out and clasp the golden ball of happiness that was dangling so close to her eyes. For one thing, she was not entirely sure she was awake and not dreaming; and for another, Georgina Islesworth couldn't possibly have wanted to release him. She was so sure of that that it was like an insurmountable barrier she could neither get round nor climb over.

She felt him relax his hold a little, and he spoke jerkily:

"Perhaps I made a mistake. Did I make a mistake? Is it Johnny's interests you've been considering all this time, and did you never once think of me as anything other than Johnny's guardian?"

"No." She could hardly believe it, but this was the truth. From the very beginning he had affected her as no other man had affected her. . . . Even while she was still fuzzy from the accident she had been aware of him, in some strange way, as a being apart from all other beings. She had been so unhappy when she thought she had to go away from him and take Johnny with her that her unhappiness had been a solid burden she had had to carry around with her.

So she looked up frankly directly into his eyes, and made her admission:

"Oh, no, no! The happiest day of my life was that other day we spent here beside the river, and when I thought it all had to end very soon. . . that, in actual fact, it had ended—"

"You were unhappy?"

Her transparent blue eyes filled with amazement.

"Unhappy? I wonder whether you know the meaning of the word?"

"Then you're a remarkably good actress!"

"So are you! I thought that the idea of settling down with Miss Islesworth filled you with a sort of contentment. I don't think I ever thought you were madly in love with her—"

"And now that you know I'm not?"

"I—I"

All at once he kissed her—full on the lips. It was a novel experience for her, because she had never been kissed by a man like that before, and something about the contact shook her to her foundations. And then he kissed her again, more gently and more lingeringly, and this time his arms closed round her.

She found that she simply hadn't the power to resist him, and there in the heart of the little wood, with the sunlight gilding the river as it flowed murmurously not many feet away, kingfishers sporting among the reeds, and Johnny—or so they imagined—still hunting for frogs, they melted into one another's arms and the man who had been willing to marry without love trembled at the thought of what he had so nearly lost, and Victoria felt bemused by what she had apparently gained.

Until Johnny came bursting in on their sanctuary and announced that he had captured a grass snake.

"Do you think we could find a box to put it in?" He was holding it up by its tail. "Or perhaps we might make it a nest in the picnic hamper...."

He stood still, staring at them, as if he honestly couldn't believe the evidence of his eyes. And then he gave one of his short, triumphant whoops.

"I read in a book that if a gentleman kisses a lady he's got to marry her," he cried. "So now you've got to marry him, Victoria, and he won't have to marry Miss Islesworth after all! Isn't it fun? Because I don't like Miss Islesworth and I do love you, Victoria... and I like Sir Peter, too."

"Thanks," Sir Peter returned, with a certain amount of dry appreciation.

CHAPTER TWELVE

THE HOMEWARD DRIVE was a revelation to Victoria. She had never known that one could feel so happy and so entirely delighted with life that there was no longer a single cloud on her horizon.

Sir Peter had talked her out of even the smallest tinge of conscience where Georgina Islesworth was concerned. If she really had thrown her ring at his feet and told him he could marry her, Victoria, then he was entirely within his rights if he took her at her word. After all, it was a serious insult in itself when a woman flung her engagement ring at the feet of the man who had given it to her, and one could hardly expect a man of Sir Peter's background and upbringing to relish being humiliated in that fashion. And if he had never been in love with Georgina, and she had never been in love with him, then the chances of their being really happy together were remote...so the fact that they had parted was a happy escape for them both.

And as Victoria, after an afternoon beside the river with the man she herself loved, could no longer doubt that he loved her quite as much as she loved him, then she would have been wilfully destroying her own happiness and his if she had persisted in championing the cause of Georgina.

So the drive back to Alder Cottage was an experience for Victoria that she knew she would never forget.

Johnny sat in the back of the car and was sufficiently diplomatic to make no complaints about being relegated once more to a seat he despised. His fingers itched to get at the controls of the big car, and he loved to watch Sir Peter manipulating the gears, but he understood with a lucidity that was extraordinary in one so young that Victoria's place was now—and until she got tired of it, anyway, or was prepared to make an occasional sacrifice—beside the man she intended to marry.

And the fact that she was going to marry him had delighted Johnny so much that he, in his turn, was a trifle bemused by the turn of events, and the rightness of everything that was happening to him.

So he sat in the back and wondered, in his childish fashion, why life that could be so unexpectedly cruel and deprive him of his rightful parent could also, a very short while afterward, unbend to such an extent that his cup of sheer childish bliss was full. It was something to marvel at, and as they sped through the lanes and the warmth of the afternoon persisted he found his head nodding from time to time, and the effort to explain matters satisfactorily to himself was so great in such a temperature that he finally fell fast asleep. And when Victoria glanced back at him she smiled because there was a look of supreme contentment on his face.

She knew that she would never experience another drive like this. There would be others—perhaps far more wonderful ones—but this one represented a gateway of promise, a door to delights hitherto undreamed of simply because she hadn't dared to dream of them.

But now Peter allowed one of his hands to desert the wheel occasionally, and it felt for hers and gripped them so strongly that she knew she was not dreaming. And sometimes he turned his eyes toward her and they just looked at one another, and she felt as if her breathing was interfered with, and every pulse in her body throbbed with happiness and wonder.

The fields and the woods sped past. They didn't actually discuss what had happened to them, and they made no plans for the future, but with past and future suspended and merged into the present it didn't matter.

In a way, Victoria realized, they were floating on unreal clouds of bliss...but at least it was bliss, and that was all that mattered.

When they arrived back at the cottage it was close upon six o'clock, and Victoria wakened Johnny, and he entered the cottage rubbing his eyes and feeling slightly bewildered. Something had happened which merited a celebration—Sir Peter was staying to supper—but he couldn't quite recall what it was at the moment.

Victoria had no need to recall anything. She trod air as she walked the length of the garden path, and she knew Peter did the same thing as he followed her.

He absolutely refused to go back to Wycherley Park for dinner, and that meant she had to provide him with an eatable meal. This wasn't such a problem, for she had well stocked her larder, and every time she glanced at Peter she felt convinced that he was no more hungry than she was. And but for the fact that Johnny had to be provided with something to eat they would probably have wandered into the garden and sat there and forgotten everything but the fact that the two of them were together.

As soon as supper was over and Johnny was in bed they did wander into the garden, and for once Victoria consented to stack the dishes and leave them for Mrs. Wavertree when she arrived the following day.

"There's one think I must make clear to you," Peter said, when they sat side by side on the white-painted garden seat and he toyed with her ringless hand. "It's absolutely true that I've never been in love before...and I'd like to be assured that you've never been in love, either."

Victoria felt amused by his craving for assurance. If only she could make him see, with her eyes, the kind of life she had led up till now! She had changed, before supper, into her light blue dress, and as the moon rose it once more acquired that quality of deli-

cacy and entire lack of substance that it had had the
night before. Unfortunately there were a few clouds
tonight, and the moon was occasionally obscured by
them, but even in the soft scented dark there was a
sort of shimmer about her, and it wasn't confined to
her hair and her dress.

"Do you want me to tell you the truth?" she
asked, looking upward through the boughs above her
head. "That I'd never even been kissed—properly,
that is," blushing under cover of the dark—"until
this afternoon. I am what you could describe as a
positive amateur."

"Thank goodness for that," Peter breathed at her
side.

She turned and looked at him a little critically.

"At least we can't say the same thing about you,"
she reminded him, astounded by the feeling of jeal-
ousy that possessed her when she thought of him with
Miss Islesworth in his arms. "For even if you were
never in love with Georgina you must have kissed her
many times!"

"Duty kisses," he responded, freeing one of his
hands in order to light himself a cigarette.

She frowned.

"And was Georgina content with them?"

He shrugged.

"If she wasn't content she never reproached me. I
think we both accepted that passionate lovemaking
was out—where we two were concerned, at any rate.
Naturally, as I've said before, I admire her, and it

wasn't exactly unpleasant making a form of light love to her...."

Victoria bit her lip.

"Could you do it again?" she demanded. "After—after kissing me?"

"Making violent love to you, you mean." He reached out and snatched her into his arms, and for one moment she forgot everything while his mouth covered hers and his arms held her. The knowledge that she could turn her head toward him and nestle it into his shoulder was sheer bliss... and even while discussing with him the relative merits of lovemaking that was inspired by nothing more than a desire to be cooperative and lovemaking that was purely and simply the result of deep compulsion, she was only too happy to avail herself of the advantages bestowed upon her by her new status.

Sir Peter stroked her hair a little reproachfully.

"No, I couldn't kiss her again."

"And you're quite—quite sure about—us?"

He put his fingers beneath her chin and lifted it, and the moonlight poured into her eyes as it broke free from a cloud.

She felt his long fingers gently massaging her throat.

"If I was not sure," he demanded huskily, "would I be here with you now?"

The hours passed, and the moon climbed high in the sky. The nightingale inhabiting the nearby thicket started tuning up about eleven o'clock, and a quarter of an hour later was distilling magic and scattering it on the otherwise absolute stillness and quiet of the night, as if it was some sort of commodity reserved for the delectation of those fortunates dwelling in such a place.

Victoria, who had listened to it often, was bemused by it tonight. The concert lasted for about half an hour, and then silence settled down over the cottage and the garden. Peter said regretfully that he must tear himself away and allow her to go to bed, but when the actual moment of separation came Victoria realized that they still hadn't made any plans for the future. They had sat enthralled by their surroundings and murmured to one another occasionally, but that was all they had done. And as soon as she was alone the various omissions occurred to her, and she tried to reassure herself about them because, after all, until a few hours before she had never expected to be engaged to marry Sir Peter . . . and he, up until twenty-four hours before, had been engaged to someone else.

So she could hardly expect him to free his mind of all previous entanglements so suddenly and start off on an entirely new track making plans for their joint future.

In any case—and once she was alone to fully realize her happiness—she knew she had more than enough to occupy her for the present without bothering about the future, not even the immediate future.

Sir Peter had said he would be with her the following day, and that was as far as they had gone in the matter of looking ahead.

Once she had said good-night to him, and as on the night before he had waited outside the door of the cottage until she locked and bolted it, she went straight upstairs to her room and curled herself up in an armchair beside the window, for she was far too excited and emotionally "lit up" to go to bed. Johnny, in the next room, slumbered peacefully, and the cottage was very quiet. With her arms about her drawn-up knees and her eyes on the starry firmament that spread itself above the tangled boughs outside her window, she relived every moment of the evening just passed, as well as a good many moments during the day...and the dawn light was invading the sky when she finally went to bed.

She wondered whether Peter, not so far away at Wycherley Park, was doing the same thing at around about the same hour. Or whether, being a man, he was more practical and had long since gone to bed and was probably fast asleep—and, she could only hope, dreaming of her when she at last slid between the sheets.

The next morning, despite the hour at which her head touched the pillow, she was up early and had the breakfast table laid and the grill switched on ready for making toast shortly after half past seven. Every instinct she possessed warned her that Sir Peter would arrive at any moment, and he would certainly want breakfast, and, equally certainly, a substantial one.

As for herself, she couldn't do more than swallow a cup of coffee, and even the piece of toast she buttered for herself was left untasted.

Johnny came down about eight o'clock, looking very suntanned as a result of his long day in the open the day before. He took his place at the table and looked at the extra set of cutlery that had been laid out on the snowy cloth, but he offered no comment, although his eyes went somewhat searchingly to Victoria's face.

"I heard you moving about in the night," he said. "Didn't you go to bed?"

Victoria reassured him, ruffling his hair lightly as she passed behind his chair.

"Oh, yes, I went to bed. But you'd been asleep a long time when I did," she told him, smiling at him.

Johnny looked as if he was recollecting something of importance.

"You couldn't sleep," he accused her.

Victoria agreed with him complacently.

"No, I couldn't," she admitted. "But I'm fresh as a daisy this morning," she added.

Johnny's eyes were unable to detect any harrowing effects of her sleepless night. On the contrary, her eyes were as bright and her skin was as radiant as the early morning itself. She was wearing a dress he hadn't seen before—a crisp print she had made herself, and because it had a lot of blue in it was entirely right for her—and her golden hair was caught up in a ponytail by means of a light blue ribbon.

With a small apron round her middle and an immaculate frying pan in her hands, she looked, he thought, almost good enough to eat herself.

Victoria buttered him some toast, cooked his egg and placed it in front of him, and then stood behind her own chair with her eyes wandering constantly in the direction of the window. And Johnny immediately remembered what he simply couldn't understand he hadn't remembered earlier.

"Sir Peter!" he exclaimed, waving the marmalade spoon. "You're expecting him for breakfast! You're going to marry him and he's going to spend a lot of time with us here at the cottage.... Until you do marry him, I mean!"

Victoria didn't deny the imputation, but she urged him to get on with his breakfast.

"And then you can give Sir Peter's car a rub with one of my brand new dusters," she told him.

Johnny's eyes gleamed at this—he was going through a phase when cars of all kinds (but preferably smart new expensive ones!) were an obsession with him. As soon as he had disposed of his last mouthful of toast he went out into the garden and stationed himself at the gate to watch for Sir Peter. It wasn't quite such a bright and brilliant morning, but it was fine enough, full of the right amount of promise.

Johnny, in a clean T-shirt and very short shorts, hung over the garden gate and strained his eyes to catch the very earliest possible glimpse he could catch of Sir Peter and the Bentley; but he was still doing the same thing when an hour had passed, and by that time Victoria had joined him at the gate.

She was still keeping the top of the stove hot, but she had washed up her own and Johnny's breakfast things, and the chimes of the village church clock—which reached them on a still morning—informed her that it was now nine o'clock.

If Peter was coming to breakfast something must have held him up.

When the church clock chimed ten they were still leaning on the garden gate, but Johnny was growing restless. Victoria dismissed him from his post and urged him to go and dig in the garden, or do something to divert himself. Mrs. Wavertree arrived and removed the immaculate cloth from the kitchen table, and Victoria was forced to face up to the knowledge that Peter would not now require breakfast when he arrived.

Mrs. Wavertree was in a very chatty mood, and Victoria followed her indoors and discussed local affairs with her. She wished to appear as normal as possible, and she had already cautioned Johnny that he must say nothing at all of what had occurred the day before.

For the moment, at any rate, the happenings of the day before were a secret between herself, Sir Peter and Johnny.

Johnny seemed to think this a little odd, but he was ever ready to oblige. If a secret had to be kept he was the very one to keep it, and he went round making mysterious observations about the table being cleared, and hinting very broadly to Mrs. Wavertree that they would probably have a visitor to lunch.

But eleven o'clock came, and twelve o'clock, and there was still no Sir Peter. The butcher's boy brought chops for lunch, and Mrs. Wavertree sliced the beans and did the potatoes. Victoria went outside into the kitchen garden and picked the last of the loganberries, and afterwards she made them into a tart and made absolutely certain there was cream in the fridge to go with them.

"If there isn't, I can go to the village and get some," Johnny offered. But it wasn't necessary. There was cream.

Mrs. Wavertree departed at half-past twelve, and by that time Victoria was feeling unreasonably desperate. Why didn't Peter come? And since he hadn't come, what was keeping him? When he departed the night before he had said quite distinctly, "See you tomorrow morning." And now it was no longer morning. It was afternoon.

Victoria cooked the lunch and served it at the usual time, feeling, while she dished up the vegetables, as if she could cry into the vegetable water that drained from the colander. This, she knew, was absurd, because anything could have kept Peter, and the fact that her hands were shaking and she fumbled with everything she did was a sign of unreasonable nervous tension she was ashamed of, but which she couldn't combat.

For a moment she thought of telephoning to Wycherley Park—until the thought that she might be suspected of running after him stopped her.

By three o'clock in the afternoon she was quite sure that Sir Peter had been involved in an accident, and when teatime came without him putting in an appearance she was absolutely convinced of it. Nevertheless, she did her best to prevent this dire feeling communicating itself to Johnny. As he was restless after tea and wandered about with his hands in the pockets of his shorts, kicking up stones and scowling at the paved walk, she decided that the two of them would have to go for a brief walk, and when they returned perhaps they would find Peter leaning on the gate and waiting for them.

This picture comforted her all the way along an abandoned car track and over a muddy field; and it was still bright and offering her a good deal of consolation even after she and Johnny had wandered in their favorite beech wood and collected several varieties of ferns to take back to the cottage. But before the white garden gate came in sight she knew Peter was not at the cottage.

For there was no sign of his car in the lane.

Johnny went to bed at six o'clock, and Victoria went outside again to do some determined gardening, and grubbed about in the earth until her hands were badly stained, since she had neglected to put on gardening gloves, and one or two thorns had been driven into her fingers and she had been badly stung by nettles.

Then, when it was growing dusk, she went indoors and switched on the radio and the desk lamp, then sat down and stared in a defeated fashion at the farther wall.

Peter was not coming. Something had gone wrong, or else he had forgotten that he had promised to come, and that in its way was even more serious than something going wrong.

Not that she wanted anything to happen to the man who was now her whole life and future existence. But it was dreadful to think that he might, after all, have forgotten his first serious promise to her, and when she saw him again he would simply say casually that he had forgotten.

She put her hands up to her face and clutched at it in anguish as she sat there torturing herself.

She knew she was torturing herself, but what else could she do, alone there in the cottage?

The fact that Johnny was upstairs asleep was no real comfort. She adored Johnny, and she wanted him to have a restful night, but if only he was older—and preferably a woman of experience—and she could have talked to him. Johnny was in many ways so shrewd and practical. He might have issued her some sound advice if she had taken him into her confidence before he went upstairs to his room...and as a result of that advice she might now be feeling more comforted.

There were even moments during that long, long evening when she actually made for the foot of the stairs in order to wake Johnny and take him into her confidence. But common sense, and her paramount desire not to disturb him, prevailed in the end, and she retained her seat before the hearth, on which instead of coals a vase of flowers lit up the cavernous space, and the scent of them filled the room.

At ten o'clock she went outside and walked desperately up and down the garden path in fitful moonlight for about half an hour. . .and then she turned to go back indoors again, for there was not even a nightingale singing in the wood to divert her tonight.

But there was the sound of a car coming along the lane.

She fairly raced to the gate to welcome Peter, all her fears and thoughts scattered to the winds, her eyes shining like the brightest of bright stars in the heavens above her.

CHAPTER THIRTEEN

GEORGINA STEPPED from the car with a grace that betokened a natural assurance and ease; but there was no hostility in her face as she approached the gate.

Victoria could have cried aloud with disappointment when she saw that the car that stopped at the gate was not the familiar, sleek gray Bentley, but a gleaming affair of almost startling white. Against the background of shadows crowding close in the lane it seemed to her to have an almost unearthly pallor.

Georgina said sympathetically:

"Poor Miss Wood! Are you still hoping against hope that Sir Peter will turn up?"

Victoria stared without making any answer.

Georgina opened the gate herself and stood on the flagged path beside Victoria looking critically and a trifle contemptuously around the sleeping garden of the cottage. The light from the sitting-room window streamed out across the lawn, and it all looked very serene and peaceful and a trifle unreal against the setting of darkness.

Victoria managed to find her voice.

"Is—is anything wrong?" In her own ears her voice sounded husky to the point of being barely audible. "With—with Sir Peter?"

Georgina smiled at her with just a touch of open contempt.

"Not a thing, my dear! Why should there be? Things don't happen easily to a man like Sir Peter Wycherley. He's rich enough to combat most of the evils of life, and he's always been extraordinarily fortunate so far as I know. No; there's nothing wrong. It's simply that he sent me to see you."

"Why?"

Georgina shrugged. She was wearing a thin silk coat over a pale silk dress—wild silk, since Georgina preferred it to any other variety—and although the night drained the color out of it Victoria would have been prepared to swear that it was wild-rose pink, or possibly lilac. However, she was not in any mood to swear to anything just then, and she merely noted the details of the outfit out of the corner of her eye. And Georgina's beguiling darkness and bewitching, flawless skin awakened a purely temporary feeling of admiration that she was not aware of herself.

Georgina advanced toward the cottage.

"Can't we go inside?" she suggested. "I didn't exactly contemplate having a kind of heart-to-heart with you in the open."

Victoria acquiesced without saying a word. She knew that something was worse than wrong...not, apparently, with Sir Peter Wycherley, but with her world. In the next few seconds it was going to collapse in ruins about her ears. And in order that she shouldn't betray her abject vulnerability and the sickening disappointment and bewilderment that was already turning her completely cold inside, she maintained her silence until she had closed the door on the two of them and switched on another wall light to add to the revealing illumination.

Then, and then only, did Georgina turn and look at her.

"You must believe me when I tell you that I'm sorry for you," she said. "But you ought to have had more sense from the beginning. You shouldn't have expected such a lot from any man. Least of all Peter! He's a charmer, and I adore him, but I understand perfectly his greatest weakness."

Victoria licked her lips.

"What is that?"

"Kindness, a desire to be generous all the time. He simply can't bear to see anyone frustrated or in need of pity or sympathy, and in the case of the boy Johnny I understood perfectly why he wanted to do things for him. The child was rendered fatherless and he hasn't any mother, so why shouldn't he adopt him? It was the logical thing for him to do according to his lights. Then there was you...."

Once more Victoria licked her lips.

"What about me?"

"You're such a pathetic little thing, and you made it so obvious that you fell for him right from the outset.'' She was pacing up and down in the living room of the cottage, lifting ornaments and examining them idly, picking up books and discarding them. She came to the new transistor radio and smiled as she touched it. ''A present for Johnny?''

The other girl nodded. She was very white under the lights, and in an extraordinary, detached manner she was forcing herself to accept the discovery that Miss Islesworth's coat and dress were actually pale lavender, and not lilac or pink. It was almost a bluish lavender, in fact. And with her satin-smooth hair and her slumbrous dark glances it was wonderfully attractive.

''Well, shall we get to the point?''

Without being invited to do so she sank down in a chair.

''I must say, you're very comfortable here...very comfortable.'' A gleam of something that was not at all slumbrous appeared in her eyes. ''You really have dug yourself in, haven't you? You and the child! No wonder the whole district is talking.''

''Talking?''

Georgina subjected her to a glance of amazement.

''But did it never once occur to you that people would talk? And in the country people talk louder and faster than anywhere else. Scandal just spreads like a forest fire...and in this case I must say you deserved it. But poor Peter hasn't really deserved to be talked about...after all, he meant well, and he certainly meant nothing underhand. So we'll just have to do what we can to correct the unpleasant rumors when we hear them.''

Victoria felt as if she was being deliberately played with and kept on tenderhooks.

''Are you trying to tell me,'' she asked, moistening her lips with the tip of her tongue, ''that you've come here with the consent and approval of Sir Peter Wycherley?''

Miss Islesworth took a moment or two to consider this, then gave an emphatic nod of the head which sent all Victoria's hopes of future happiness descending into a lost world of abandoned hopes and blighted prospects.

''Well, do you honestly think I would come here at this late hour if I was acting entirely on my own initiative?'' the dark girl counter-questioned. ''After all—'' with a smile which belied her words ''—I'm not entirely heartless, and I do realize that you're very innocent and have probably been led up the garden path, in a kind of way. Yes, Peter was so upset about the whole thing getting so badly out of hand that I had to do something tonight . . . and, as a matter of fact, I've come here straight from Wycherley Park, where he's pacing up and down in his library like a badly concerned tiger . . . not a vicious one, but an anxious one. I do hope you'll believe me when I say he never meant you any harm!''

Victoria recoiled as if she had received an actual slap across the face.

''He couldn't even come and . . . tell me himself?''

"He thought it would be less painful—for both of you!—if I did. We discussed it over dinner, and over coffee afterward, and then I made the decision to come here. Yes, the decision was actually mine, but Peter agreed to it. He was, as a matter of fact, almost pathetically relieved."

This was something Victoria found it difficult to believe, with her knowledge of Sir Peter. But if he was capable of wilfully deceiving both her and Johnny, without any real reason why he should stoop to such duplicity, then he was capable of almost anything.

"What—do you want me to do?" she asked, her throat very dry.

Georgina shrugged, but looked at her with sympathy at the same time.

"Well, if it was me," she said, as if she had given a great deal of thought to this piece of advice, and rehearsed her reply in advance, "I would pack up and leave here without delay. I believe you tried to get away before, but Peter stopped you. This time you mustn't let him interfere with your plans. Remember that it's humiliating to be dealt with as you have been dealt with, and in addition you must be feeling pretty sore...with Peter, I mean. You don't want to involve yourself in recriminations—and I know it's the last thing Peter wants, because of his guilty conscience—and you do want to save some remnants of your pride. Get away while you can, and before his conscience starts troubling him afresh, and he comes here to apologize personally." She looked aghast at the prospect. "That's something I know I couldn't stand, and I don't suppose you feel much differently. Do take my advice and get away either tonight or tomorrow morning. There's a good train in the morning, so I should wait until then. You can order a taxi tonight to pick you up first thing in the morning."

"How will I order a taxi?" Victoria sounded as someone other than herself was speaking. "We're not on the village telephone here."

"Then I'll order one for you myself. I know a very good man who'll pick you up about seven o'clock and get you to the junction in good time to find seats on the train. It's going to be a bit of a rush for you, but unless you prefer to face up to a possible ordeal...."

"No, no, I'll go!"

"And I'll order the taxi for you."

Miss Islesworth rose.

"I think you're being awfully sensible about this—" Victoria wondered afterward whether she had expected a scene—defiance, perhaps, or at any rate proof of what she said. But Victoria felt she had received proof enough, otherwise Peter would have kept his word and been there in the morning. "I won't hold you up now, because you've got all your packing to do. But anything you want...well—" she handed over a slip of pasteboard which she had removed from her handbag "—that's the address of my

London flat, where I shall be in a week's time. And if you find yourself up against it, or need help in finding either living quarters or some sort of a job, just ring me, and I'll make an appointment to see you. I'm perfectly certain I'll be able to help you.''

''Thank you,'' Victoria acknowledged the offer, tonelessly.

Having delivered herself of the reason for her late visit, Miss Islesworth seemed anxious to depart. She walked quickly to the door and let herself out, and as Victoria followed her mechanically down the garden path she waved her back.

''No, don't bother to see me to my car.'' There was something beautifully poised and condescending about her attitude, despite her expressed sympathy. ''I know you've got a lot to do. Don't let me hold you up.''

Victoria listened to her footsteps retreating down the flagged path of the cottage, and when she judged that the visitor was inside her car, she closed the front door of the cottage and bolted it automatically. Then she went upstairs to Johnny's room and stood looking down at him with an utterly expressionless look on her face.

She didn't go to bed that night. She made herself some tea and then started packing her own and Johnny's things. While she did so, she forced her mind to become a blank. Every move she made was an effort and required a conscious effort of will. For hours she felt like someone who had had all the life drained out of her, and was responding simply to some inner compulsive voice. But she managed to preserve the cotton-wool condition that had enveloped her thinking powers, and could not honestly have said afterwards if she was either deathly miserable or temporarily distracted while she did an efficient job of packing.

It was so efficient that she very soon had everything ready and waiting in the hall. Then she went from room to room of the cottage, making absolutely certain that everything was tidy, and in order, as she had found it. The fact that she had no intention of sleeping in her bed enabled her to strip it and fold the sheets and arrange the blankets neatly under the bed covers. Johnny's room would have to wait until he was up, but she knew it wouldn't take her long.

She left the flowers in the sitting-room vases, because it seemed a pity to throw them away.... But everything else was in apple-pie order long before the first cockerel in the district started crowing, and the mists of dawn started rising from the surrounding meadows.

At five o'clock she made herself another pot of tea, watched the sun rise redly over the garden, climbed the stairs like someone about to undertake a most unpleasant task and aroused Johnny.

She had decided to say nothing about the reason for leaving, apart from giving him to understand that they had to leave—later, perhaps, she would tell him

a little of the truth—and he had always been an unusually easy child (in difficult moments) to manage.
Apart from gazing wide-eyed he asked no questions,
and therefore it was quite unnecessary to tell him any
half truths.

This morning, as always, he ate a hearty breakfast,
and afterward she washed up the breakfast things
and put them away, then ran the carpet sweeper over
the sitting-room carpet in order that it should be left
immaculate.

Then Johnny went out to the garden to say goodbye to some favorite bird friends, and release a toad
that he had been trying to tame. He gazed regretfully
at his small corner of the garden where the flowers
that were thriving had been looked after by himself,
and picked one or two of them to take away with
him.

He was returning to the house when the car shot
round the bend of the lane and drew up with a faint
screech of brakes outside the cottage gate. Peter
Wycherley left the driving seat with the impatience of
one who had already made a good deal of hurry that
morning, and called out to Johnny when he caught
sight of him.

"You're up early, Johnny! Couldn't you sleep?"

Johnny, in his best tussore silk shirt and well-
pressed contrasting shorts—to say nothing of immaculate socks and shoes—turned and stared at him.

"We're going away," he said.

"Oh!" Sir Peter thrust open the gate, and looked at him grimly. "Where's Victoria?" he asked.

"Inside."

"Stay here while I talk to her," his guardian ordered.

CHAPTER FOURTEEN

VICTORIA WAS in the kitchen when Peter entered the cottage. He was so used to finding his way about in the cottage by now that he walked straight in on her, and although he didn't say anything she knew at once that he was standing there looking at her.

She hadn't heard his car stop at the gate. She hadn't heard his footsteps on the path. Why she hadn't done so she could never afterward quite understand, unless the truth was that she was in such a state of acute depression and strange mental inertia that she was deaf to everything that was going on around her. She was like someone moving in a dream no longer with any expectations of life, and with nothing but a dreary future ahead of her. She wasn't even agitated by all that she had to cope with, and the responsibilities that would be hers in the future.

But, as soon as Sir Peter arrived in the kitchen doorway, she knew. She was giving the stove a final careful wipe, and she turned with the damp cloth in her hand to confront him.

"Good morning," he said, with a kind of arctic coldness.

Victoria dropped the damp cloth. He stooped politely and picked it up for her.

"Where do you want this?" he asked, and cast it into the sink before she had time to answer. "You shouldn't be doing kitchen chores in your best traveling suit," he observed crisply. "You might spoil it."

She couldn't think of anything to say to answer him. She was wondering what he was doing there at that hour, and could only conclude that he had undergone a change of mind...and, possibly, heart. But they were only temporary changes, of course.

"Johnny, too, seems to be wearing his best," he continued conversationally. "He tells me you're going away."

At that she managed to admit that Johnny was right.

"Yes; we're going away," she said.

"Where to? Not London? It's usually London with you, isn't it?"

A temporary indignation flared up in her eyes.

"Where else would I go with Johnny when I have to find a job to support him?" she demanded.

He shrugged his tweed-clad shoulders slightly.

"You could try Manchester or Birmingham, or even Edinburgh. Edinburgh isn't much farther from here than London is. In fact, it isn't as far."

He advanced to the kitchen table and set down a very small, beautifully wrapped paper package on it. It looked ridiculously small by comparison with the size of the table, and Victoria gazed at it in slight astonishment.

"What is it?" she said.

Sir Peter backed toward the door.

"It's for you," he told her, in a colorless tone. "But you don't have to open it now. In the train, perhaps, when you and Johnny are comfortably settled in your second-class carriage. After that you can pawn it or sell it, or even throw it away if you'd rather do that. So long as you don't return it to me, since I've no desire whatsoever to see it again, I don't mind. I made a journey to London to get it, and thought I'd broken all records getting back here in time to breakfast with you this morning; but apparently you haven't any breakfast to offer me...not even a welcome! So I'll see if the cook can do better at the Park. At any rate, she's not in a position to refuse me breakfast," and he turned on his heel and swung out through the door.

Victoria raced after him and clutched at his sleeve.

"What do you mean? Broken all records?" she demanded breathlessly.

He glanced at her almost disdainfully.

"Does it matter?" he inquired icily. "Don't let me make you miss your train. I believe I hear a taxi coming along the lane. Is that yours?"

"I—er—yes."

"Then don't keep the driver waiting. He's probably got other fares besides you this morning."

And he actually shook off her hand and walked at lightning speed away down the garden path.

Victoria, awakened almost rudely out of her lethargy, and saved from the very brink of a slough of despond, was completely uncertain about what to do next...to race after him, or to open the package. Undoubtedly the package contained the answer to a riddle, but she had already read the answer to the riddle in Peter Wycherley's face, and she knew that if she paused long enough to open the package she would lose him for good. She had probably lost him already, but she had to find out...to put her fate to this final test. So, snatching up the package and grabbing Johnny by the hand as she passed him on the garden path, she flew down the path to the gate, and saw Sir Peter's car shoot away from it just as the local taxi rolled to a halt outside it and the local taximan descended from his perch and greeted her with all the affability in the wordl.

"Good morning, miss!" He touched his cap to her. "The lady said I was to be on time so that you wouldn't miss the train. Lovely morning, isn't it? Seems a pity you're going away."

Victoria addressed him breathlessly.

"Catch that car," she said. She cast a glance of agonized dubiousness at the ancient taxi. "Do you think you can possibly managed to catch up with it? It's Sir Peter Wycherley's car! You must!" she added imploringly.

The taximan looked as dubious as her glance, but he agreed to have a good try.

"It's surprising, sometimes, what the old girl can

do," he said. "Just you hang on to your seats, miss, and we'll see what we can do!"

Sir Peter, most unfortunately, had a good start. And as, despite the bends in the lane—distinctly treacherous bends, Victoria realized, as they followed in pursuit—he was pressing his foot and his accelerator and getting all the speed he could out of a highly powerful car there seemed little hope that they would ever catch him up.

But the taximan had once driven in a rally, away back in his youth, and he got the excitement of the chase in his veins. He gave the antiquated vehicle its head, and they roared along the lanes in hot pursuit of the sleek and glistening Bentley, until Sir Peter suddenly realized that a determined and highly dangerous attempt was being made to catch up with him and drew into the side of the road and kindly, but with a face of granite, allowed them to draw alongside—thus effectively blocking the road.

Sir Peter spoke briefly.

"If you don't want to be cut off in your prime," he advised the grinning taximan, "you'll allow your passengers to come in here and get on your way." He held open the rear door of the Bentley, but Johnny scrambled triumphantly into the vacant seat beside him. Victoria, still clutching her precious package, subsided on to the rear seat, and knew that she was trembling all over—partly with excitement, partly with inexpressible relief.

"Send your bill to me," Sir Peter ordered, and the

other man touched his peaked cap to him. His highly gratified expression stated that it was completely all right by him.

"The lady said catch up with you, and I caught up with you, sir," he revealed.

Sir Peter simply looked astonished.

As soon as the taxi had gone on its way Sir Peter turned and looked inquiringly at the girl on the back seat of his car.

"The station?" he inquired coldly.

She shook her head.

"No, please. I want to talk to you, Peter," she begged humbly. "Can't we go somewhere where we can...talk?"

"Back to the cottage?"

"It's as good a place as any."

"Very well."

He turned the car, and in the space of a very few minutes they were back at the little white gate set in the high hedge, and Johnny was urged to scramble out with as much speed as he had scrambled in. He looked acutely disappointed at first, until Sir Peter, after ordering him to make himself scarce for a short while, comforted him by promising to take him for a drive in the Bentley later on.

"When Miss Wood has handed you over to my custody," he said with a good deal of grimness, and Johnny glanced at him in fresh alarm. But something about Sir Peter's expression—despite its grimness—reassured him, and he ran off happily to find out whether his toad had wandered very far after all, and to recapture it if possible and provide it with its favorite lettuce leaf breakfast.

But Victoria knew she had transgressed far beyond the bounds of being easily forgiven. She and Peter remained in the garden, and it wasn't until he invited her that she dared to join him in the seat beside the driving seat. He noticed she was still holding on tightly to the package he had flung down on the kitchen table.

"So you haven't opened it," he said.

"No."

"Have you the least idea what's inside it?"

She didn't make the mistake of shaking her head. It was, in a way, such an obvious package.

"I think it's something small," she said.

"It's a sapphire and diamond ring." He turned and looked at her coolly . . . so coolly that she turned cold, despite the fact that it was already a beautiful morning. "An engagement ring. But I take it you no longer contemplate becoming engaged to me?"

Her blue eyes looked haunted, and utterly unhappy. She knew if she told him that she had been taking herself and Johnny away simply because the woman he had once been engaged to had told her a series of deliberate untruths he would despise her. He would never be able to trust her, or believe in the quality of her love.

And yet—since it was the truth—what else could she tell him?

She licked her lips, swallowed convulsively, took a deep breath...and was about to admit to the truth when he laid a hand firmly and comfortingly over both of her.

"It's all right, darling," he said, softly. "In a way, I'm the one to blame. I didn't actually ask you to marry me, and Georgina said she would smash things up between us. I take it that she had a good try?"

In a mortified voice she whispered:

"Yes."

He smiled at her—tenderly, and with complete understanding. After all, she was such a slip of a thing, and she had no real idea how important she was to him. She had a kind of natural humility which made it easy for someone full of self confidence like Georgina Islesworth to get at her and undermine what little self-confidence she had completely.

He squeezed her hand so tightly that she winced, and then he slid an arm along the seat and drew her to him. In a slightly muffled voice, with his lips against her hair, he ordered her to open the package and try the ring on for size, and when they discovered that it fitted perfectly and her blue eyes gazed at him wonderingly he took her face between his hands and looked at her as if the sun was actually rising at the backs of his eyes.

"You like it?" he asked. "I went to London for it because I wanted something as near perfect as I could possibly get for you."

"Oh, Peter!" she breathed.

"But if I'd had the least idea you'd come hurtling after me as you did in that ancient taxi I'd have contented myself with giving you something that could have been bought locally, and then you wouldn't have had to risk life and limb. Was it a bone-shaking experience?"

She nodded, with her head against his shoulder.

"It was an experience I'll never forget," she said.

"Nor I." There was a sudden laugh in his voice. "And I don't suppose Johnny will, either!"

![Harlequin logo]

Harlequin

COLLECTION
EDITIONS OF 1978

Harlequin's Collection 1...

ANDREA BLAKE
Night of
the Hurrica...

Harlequin's Collection 106 · 1.25

ANNE WEALE
If This
Is Love

**50 great stories
of special beauty
and significance**

$1.25
each novel

In 1976 we introduced the first 100 Harlequin Collections—a selection of titles chosen from our best sellers of the past 20 years. This series, a trip down memory lane, proved how great romantic fiction can be timeless and appealing from generation to generation. The theme of love and romance is eternal, and, when placed in the hands of talented, creative, authors whose true gift lies in their ability to write from the heart, the stories reach a special level of brilliance that the passage of time cannot dim. Like a treasured heirloom, an antique of superb craftsmanship, a beautiful gift from someone loved—these stories too, have a special significance that transcends the ordinary. **$1.25 each novel**

Here are your 1978
Harlequin Collection Editions...

102 Then Come Kiss Me
MARY BURCHELL (#422)

103 It's Wise to Forget
ELIZABETH HOY (#507)

104 The Gated Road
JEAN S. MACLEOD (#547)

105 The Enchanting Island
KATHRYN BLAIR (#766)

106 If This is Love
ANNE WEALE (#798)

107 Love is Forever
BARBARA ROWAN (#799)

108 Amber Five
BETTY BEATY (#824)

109 The Dream and the Dancer
ELEANOR FARNES (#912)

110 Dear Intruder
JANE ARBOR (#919)

111 The Garden of Don José
ROSE BURGHLEY (#928)

112 Bride in Flight
ESSIE SUMMERS (#913)

113 Tiger Hall
ESTHER WYNDHAM (#936)

114 The Enchanted Trap
KATE STARR (#951)

115 A Cottage in Spain
ROSALIND BRETT (#952)

116 Nurse Madeline of Eden Grove
MARJORIE NORRELL (#962)

117 Came a Stranger
CELINE CONWAY (#965)

118 The Wings of the Morning
SUSAN BARRIE (#967)

119 Time of Grace
SARA SEALE (#973)

120 The Night of the Hurricane
ANDREA BLAKE (#974)

121 Flamingoes on the Lake
ISOBEL CHACE (#976)

122 Moon Over Africa
PAMELA KENT (#983)

123 Island in the Dawn
AVERIL IVES (#984)

124 Lady in Harley Street
ANNE VINTON (#985)

125 Play the Tune Softly
AMANDA DOYLE (#1116)

126 Will You Surrender?
JOYCE DINGWELL (#1179)

127 Towards the Dawn
JANE ARBOR (#474)

128 Love is my Reason
MARY BURCHELL (#494)

129 Strange Recompense
CATHERINE AIRLIE (#511)

130 White Hunter
ELIZABETH HOY (#577)

131 Gone Away
MARJORIE MOORE (#659)

132 Flower for a Bride
BARBARA ROWAN (#845)

133 Desert Doorway
PAMELA KENT (#909)

134 My Dear Cousin
CELINE CONWAY (#934)

135 A House for Sharing
ISOBEL CHACE (#935)

136 The House by the Lake
ELEANOR FARNES (#942)

137 Whisper of Doubt
ANDREA BLAKE (#944)

138 Islands of Summer
ANNE WEALE (#948)

139 The Third Uncle
SARA SEALE (#949)

140 Young Bar
JANE FRAZER (#958)

141 Crane Castle
JEAN S. MACLEOD (#966)

142 Sweet Brenda
PENELOPE WALSH (#968)

143 Barbary Moon
KATHRYN BLAIR (#972)

144 Hotel Mirador
ROSALIND BRETT (#989)

145 Castle Thunderbird
SUSAN BARRIE (#997)

146 Magic Symphony
ELEANOR FARNES (#998)

147 A Change for Clancy
AMANDA DOYLE (#1085)

148 Thank you, Nurse Conway
MARJORIE NORRELL (#1097)

149 Postscript to Yesterday
ESSIE SUMMERS (#1119)

150 Love in the Wilderness
DOROTHY RIVERS (#1163)

151 A Taste for Love
JOYCE DINGWELL (#1229)

Original Harlequin Romance numbers in brackets

ORDER FORM
Harlequin Reader Service

In U.S.A.
MPO Box 707
Niagara Falls, N.Y. 14302

In Canada
649 Ontario St.,
Stratford, Ontario, N5A 6W2

Please send me the following Harlequin Collection novels. I am enclosing my check or money order for $1.25 for each novel ordered, plus 25¢ to cover postage and handling.

☐ 102	☐ 115	☐ 128	☐ 140
☐ 103	☐ 116	☐ 129	☐ 141
☐ 104	☐ 117	☐ 130	☐ 142
☐ 105	☐ 118	☐ 131	☐ 143
☐ 106	☐ 119	☐ 132	☐ 144
☐ 107	☐ 120	☐ 133	☐ 145
☐ 108	☐ 121	☐ 134	☐ 146
☐ 109	☐ 122	☐ 135	☐ 147
☐ 110	☐ 123	☐ 136	☐ 148
☐ 111	☐ 124	☐ 137	☐ 149
☐ 112	☐ 125	☐ 138	☐ 150
☐ 113	☐ 126	☐ 139	☐ 151
☐ 114	☐ 127		

Number of novels checked @
$1.25 each = $ _____
N.Y. and N.J. residents add
appropriate sales tax $ _____

Postage and handling $ ___.25___

                                   TOTAL $ _____

NAME _____
                    (Please Print)
ADDRESS _____

CITY _____

STATE/PROV. _____

ZIP/POSTAL CODE _____

AB   ROM 2240

Offer expires June 30, 1979